THE PASSENGER SEAT

THE PASSENGER SEAT

A NOVEL

VIJAY KHURANA

BIBLIOASIS
Windsor, Ontario

FIRST EDITION
1 3 5 7 9 10 8 6 4 2

Library and Archives Canada Cataloguing in Publication
Title: The passenger seat : a novel / Vijay Khurana.
Names: Khurana, Vijay, author.
Identifiers: Canadiana (print) 20240480880 | Canadiana (ebook)
20240480899 | ISBN 9781771966306 (softcover)
ISBN 9781771966313 (EPUB)
Subjects: LCGFT: Novels.
Classification: LCC PR6111.H87 P37 2025 | DDC 823/.92—dc23

Edited by Daniel Wells
Copyedited by Rachel Ironstone
Typeset by Vanessa Stauffer
Cover designed by Zoe Norvell

PRINTED AND BOUND IN CANADA

This desire could be a form of anger
KATHY ACKER

When two men say hello on the street, one of them loses
NORMAN MAILER (apocryphal)

A COUNTRY ROAD, a steel truss bridge, the sun heating stanchion and tarmac, river and soil, and the skin of two near-naked boys, or men. Dry air carries a hint of something burning far off; alders and cottonwoods, just past their greenest, are vivid against the grey water. The boys-or-men are friends, they balance barefoot on the safety railing, they hold tight, they look at each other and down. There is nervous laughter, a preparatory flexing of knees. Fun and games, says Adam, and they step out. Before the fall, they are suspended for what seems an impossibly long time, long enough for Adam to notice the mild curve of Teddy's back, the tongue of greasy hair at his neck, his regular knots of spine. He has a mole between his shoulders that he probably doesn't even know about. They have heard each other's names for years, endured the same classrooms and joined the shifting social groups that form during breaks and on weekends. In the last few months, however, their friendship has accelerated.

They drop.

It is a long drop, though neither Teddy nor Adam knows exactly how high the bridge might be. What they do know, what everyone in their town knows, is that the river is far too shallow to jump into, except in this one spot. Here, a coincidence of nature has occurred, a pool several metres wide and deep enough to swallow a body. The hollow beneath the surface is invisible, of course, but the town's young people trust it. For a few weeks, when temperatures and weather and school vacation coincide, boys are often seen jumping from the bridge, mostly boys, even though parents and police have forbidden it. An outsider, a driver from elsewhere approaching on the road, might be alarmed by the sight, might even suspect their intention was to harm themselves, but on coming nearer would see that the figures are teenagers having fun, their truck parked neatly beside the bridge with towels spread over its hood.

As the friends fall, rocks and shallows rise to meet them, except in the darker place they have aimed for. Teddy hits the water first, feeling his toes splay. The pain is quickly overtaken by the shock of cold water. He surfaces, kicking, gulping breath. If he is hurt, he ignores the fact. He is loved, clean, ready to go again.

For Adam it is a little different: he needles himself, straight and practised. He has done this countless times. He wants to reach as deep as he can. Adam's cousin Cameron is five years older and swears he once touched the bottom. Adam has been chasing that high, that low, ever since. These days, now that he is older, he calls bullshit if Cameron ever mentions it, but secretly he believes. He wants to be able to tell the older man that he too felt sticky silt between his toes. He angles his chin and exhales as he sinks, pretending to be his own jet propeller, a submarine sounding. He is too old for this. He is eighteen and has outgrown vertigo, but until recently has not known what thrill might replace it. And he still loves the feeling of being submerged with empty lungs, giving his body no option but to wait until it breaks the surface. As he rises he opens his eyes, the light coming to meet him. His chest is hot and full of something that cannot be air.

They stroke and then wade to the bank, breathing sharply. Even at this time of year, the water is melted snow. Their clothes are in Adam's truck up on the shoulder. They step over sharp gravel and take the hill in their boxers, river running from their bodies. Both are lean, Adam perhaps more muscled but Teddy taller and less pale. The gel has run from Adam's hair; when he rubs his face his fingers come away sticky. Both of them privately hope someone will drive past and notice them occupying the space beside the bridge. A woman especially, or a carload of girls from school, or even one of the boys with his mom. They crave witness, someone who will remember seeing them wet and shining in the summer sun. As he navigates a boulder, Teddy feels a weird, numb heat at his left little toe. The foot's going to swell, but not until later tonight, not until they've jumped off several more times and drunk Adam's bourbon on the truck's warm hood, not until Teddy is falling asleep in his bed or on the couch in Adam's bedroom, depending on which way the evening takes them.

Only a logging truck crosses the bridge as they reach their towels, the driver too high in his cab to be seen. Even so, Teddy straightens his posture and wipes what might have been discomfort from his face. Something metallic claps slowly and repeatedly as the truck's bulk fills and then exits the bridge. Before they speak Teddy and Adam watch its twin taillights disappearing around the next bend. Its trailer is empty; loaded ones are too heavy, and not allowed to come this way.

THE SIGN OUTSIDE Adam's house calls his dad a boatbuilder, but everyone knows Michael Velum hasn't been that for a long time. What he is is a failure. He has a messy comb-over the colour of come and wet eyes with which he tells the world he has given up. Teddy sometimes thinks those eyes are trying to warn him not to have anything to do with his son, as though he has given up on Adam too. Michael takes no joy in anything Teddy can see. Having been an enthusiastic drinker, he has subsided into mute anger and banned alcohol from his house. He works at a marine supply place in the next town, but that closes November to March, during which time Adam says his dad delivers pizza at night and spends the days in his freezing workshop, listening to the radio and not building shit. A couple of times when they've been smoking, Teddy has wanted to order from Colbi's, but Adam has always talked him out of it. Now Teddy knows it's because Adam is afraid his dad might show up on the porch with the food. These were delicate things to admit; they might be dangerous in the wrong hands, and Teddy was pleased to be trusted with them. When the moment is right, he will gladly offer his own parents' secrets in return.

The room smells like burned meat. Michael Velum scrapes equal portions onto three plates, then sets them beside a potato salad on the table. As Teddy waits for his food, he imagines boy and man in the house together, just the two of them, with no female of any kind. Did Adam have to do things like clean the toilet bowl and sweep out the kitchen, things Teddy's mother reliably did? The lack of a woman makes the house seem more democratic; it appeals to Teddy despite the grim food and awkward silence while they eat. Do Adam and his father both jerk off in the same shower, one after the other?

Teddy does not know Adam's mother's name, only that she lives in the city just across the border, both close and far. Adam has not seen her in six years, and never will again. Later, once they are free of the dinner table, Teddy tells Adam that his folks are only together because splitting up would require having a conversation. He performs his pain, exaggerating partly out of sympathy for Adam and partly to warn him against assuming he is any wiser, any better. Which is not to say there is no truth to what Teddy says, especially as his mother is for sure having an affair with her friend Ron, with whom she is always *getting coffee*. She has started leaving the house in her gym clothes, Teddy has noticed. Why wear workout stuff to drink coffee? If he were still a child, he would have asked her. Now, he is careful not to ask anything at all.

Teddy still does not know whether Adam actually likes him or is just toying with him in some way. Adam has a reputation for not letting other people in on his jokes. Ceecee and her friends are half-afraid of him, but he has a generous side the others cannot see. He shares the bourbon he gets from his cousin without ever asking for cash. He never asks for gas money either. But Adam has at least one way of keeping Teddy off-balance. He offers to come by and drive him to school, which is extremely nice because the bus is a humiliation and Teddy is one of the oldest kids on it these days. But with Adam it is never a sure thing. Sometimes he will message to say he slept late or he needs to work out so won't have time to make the detour, leaving Teddy to sprint to the bus stop. Teddy has tried checking in the night before, but all he gets are replies like *should be fine, will   let u know*, with that extra space suggesting Adam had first typed something else and then deleted it. Teddy will not complain, though. He and Adam are building something, placing alternate blocks one atop the other, and he knows he cannot be the one to let the tower fall.

When it happens, driving to school with Adam sets Teddy up to enjoy the day rather than endure it. He usually gets to choose the songs, his own little radio show, though sometimes Adam puts on a podcast and keeps glancing across to make sure Teddy is listening, understanding, agreeing. Teddy prefers something with a beat, something that doesn't have to mean anything. Whenever they take a corner fast he is pushed pleasingly into his seat, a sensation like being pinned by a body that dwarfs his own. He knows Adam is showing off, but who doesn't enjoy the sound of tires just about to lose traction? Teddy does not even have his learner's permit. If it were not for Adam and the red-and-black truck, it would be the bus every day. At least he is spared that. Plus, he gets to do his own showing off. He knows Adam can see him messaging Ceecee from the passenger seat. Teddy even complains about her sometimes, in a tone that he hopes disguises his naked pride at having a girlfriend. From an early age he has been taught that to have something—a toy, a trophy—counts double if your friend has none.

ADAM FINDS IT funny, strange, uncomfortable to be around a proper family, even if Teddy's all seem to dance around one another without touching. His older sister (just a year older) is always walking into and then out of the room without saying anything. His dad is weirdly jolly about everything, in that way that makes a person seem like they're just about to snap. And his mother is weirdest of all. She told Adam to call her Elizabeth, but what reason would Adam have to use her name? Yes and No are enough, mostly. One day she said to him, Adam, take a guess why all the teaspoons in this house are plastic. Adam looked back at her like it had to be a joke. It was true, though, they were all plastic, no metal. While Teddy and his dad both grinned at the floor (Grace, the sister, wasn't there), she told him it was because the sound of a metal spoon stirring tea drove her crazy. I mean it makes me want to kill whoever's doing it, she said, smiling at her two boys, her two men. Then Elizabeth looked Adam dead in the eye and said: But then I thought, why don't I just get new spoons? Later, when they were alone in Teddy's room, Adam impersonated her saying that. Teddy looked for a moment like he was offended, then they laughed at her together. Maybe that was a test, Adam thinks now, one he didn't even know he was giving. How long has it been like that with the spoons? he asked. He could tell Teddy was deciding whether to lie. It's not such a weird thing to have a thing about, Adam added quickly. Like fingernails on the chalkboard. Except chalkboards are extinct, said Teddy. They were each holding one of Teddy's controllers, but the game was just there to make talking easier.

Maybe that was the first night Adam spent in Teddy's house, so much warmer and louder than his own. It has a constant, living hum, like the structure is breathing along with the people inside. Later, he walked to the bathroom and saw Teddy's sister sitting with her back to an open door, studying, and he wondered why anyone in their right mind would leave their bedroom open like that. For a moment he stood listening to the scratch of her highlighter, watching her bare foot flex and relax beneath the chair. Because Grace never turned around, because Adam was not caught in the act of looking, he assumed she had not sensed him there in the doorway. But when he came back from pissing the hallway was darker, and he could tell before he reached it that her door was shut. As he approached the soft light that was now escaping beneath the door, he felt briefly angry, first at himself and then at her, then a moment later these twin angers resolved into a private smile and he stepped confidently past Grace's bedroom, treading louder than he needed to.

ADAM IS BEHAVING a bit weird now. He keeps banging his knees together, hard, while they're sitting on the little couch in his room. Clothes are everywhere; there's a dull smell of sweat, and other things. Teddy is laughing, but he doesn't feel like laughing. He feels like going home, only Adam would have to drive him and he's too drunk. Or Teddy would have to call his parents to come get him, like a child. He should have asked Adam an hour ago; he could have invented a reason he had to be up early in the morning. But he has just been sitting there, paralyzed and sweating in Adam's humid bedroom. Have you and Ceecee fucked yet? Adam says suddenly. Teddy snorts. Sure, he says. Have you fucked anyone? Adam pauses, then says, That's how I got fired from Thunderbolt. Me and this girl did some things in the store room. I've never told anyone. She was older, not really a girl. Doesn't it feel weird to say *woman* though, Teddy interrupts, perhaps to give Adam the chance to end his lie before it derails. Adam pays no attention and goes on: Let's just say she had some piercings. Somebody giggles, and Teddy realizes it is him. He lowers his voice to say, That's hot though—Ceecee's going to get a tattoo. Adam doesn't ask what or where, just starts bashing his knees together again, so hard that he's shaking Teddy with the motion, nearly bumping his thigh. It is not a big couch. Teddy knows he will be sleeping here later. Summer. He's going to have to put his head either right under the shelf or where Adam's sweaty ass is now. It's probably right where he jerks off too. Of course Teddy doesn't believe Adam's story, nor does he think Adam expects him to. Adam is telling it so that Teddy will trade something about him and Ceecee. But the sex Teddy has had is not much to brag about, and he's a bad liar. Better to say nothing and make Adam imagine it. Mainly Teddy has been petrified about not pleasing Ceecee, or not pleasing her enough. There was the time she knelt between his legs in her underwear, not sex, technically, but it was probably the most excited he has ever been and would be the thing to tell if he were going to tell anything. Teddy realizes that neither of them is saying anything now. He is embarrassed and certain Adam knows what he's thinking. Luckily they are drunk, and the conversation gropes its way elsewhere. Later, when he's sober, Teddy will understand that this was a trap and will be pleased with himself for not walking into it. He will even tell Ceecee, and when she calls Adam a creep he will agree. Saying it will make him feel more mature, as though Teddy were a man and Adam just a boy. But this is wishful thinking, and there is still something in Adam that makes Teddy want to stick around, just to see what will happen.

Whatever was playing through the stereo has ended, and now Adam has started crooning, like Elvis or someone. It's not like him: he usually listens to obscure hardcore no one else has even heard of. Teddy watches him take the last mouthful of liquor then keep singing. He looks like he has forgotten Teddy is there. Another noise makes Teddy twist from the hips. He almost stands, but sinks back into the couch and looks at Adam, then at the bedroom door. Adam doesn't seem to notice, just goes on singing. The noise is human palm on flimsy wood, not a knock that says *let me in* but one that says *shut the fuck up*. Adam has a lock on his bedroom door, but Teddy can't remember if it's been turned. The empty bottle is between Adam's thighs. The lid rolled onto the floor a while ago, and neither of them bothered to pick it up. Even from the other side of the door, Adam's dad must know they're drinking. Adam's singing seems to get louder. Michael Velum's voice says: I want you two to go to sleep. It's nearly one, and some of us have to work tomorrow. The thought flashes through Teddy's mind that Adam has work tomorrow too, a shift at McDonald's. Adam swallows but keeps singing through his nose. His eyes are wet and lifeless, locked on the carpet. There is either a great hatred or a great fear in the room now. This must be the sort of thing that happens in Teddy's absence: the father at the door and the son inside, not quite obeying and not quite disobeying. Teddy can't help siding with Adam's dad, mainly because he also wants to go to sleep. And he wants water, which he can't get without leaving the room. For a few unbearable moments, nobody says anything, Michael clearly still there though not trying to open the door, Adam staring at the carpet and humming his stupid song. Teddy can't take it any longer. Sure thing, he calls out. Sorry about the noise. Footsteps then fade down the hall. Adam stops humming and looks sharply at Teddy. Fun and games, Adam says. C'mon, fuckhead, let's get out of here.

Teddy doesn't know where *fuckhead* came from, though he probably betrayed Adam by apologizing to the closed door. There's a greasy stain on the carpet. The room stinks. Above Adam's bed is an ink drawing, a kind of Manga horseman that he did himself and which Teddy has always been impressed by. What do you mean? whispers Teddy, ignoring the insult, if that's what it was. Go where? Adam yawns. Down the hall and out the door, he says. I do it all the time. Michael doesn't care what we do as long as we don't keep him awake. Adam looks like he'd pass out then and there if only he'd close his eyes. Instead he digs into his jeans and brings out the keys to the truck, shaking them like he's offering a walk to a dog. Where the fuck are we going to go, Teddy says, trying for the same venom-to-affection ratio with which Adam called him fuckhead. Adam shrugs. That's up to you, he says.

THERE IS SO much fakeness in the world, so many people willing to pretend the world is something it is not. They guard this lie like territory, like the NPC sentries in Patriot, who always stand with their backs to the thing they'll die defending. In the game, they open fire if you get too close. That is why trust is everything for Adam. Approaching the wrong person with open hands can be fatal. Somebody whose videos he watches uses Bible quotes to nail down his opinions, and one that keeps coming up is: *A whip for the horse, a bridle for the donkey, and a rod for the fool's back.* Adam likes that, just as he likes feeling that the things he knows instinctively can be proven. Most people deserve the rod, and those who don't are rare to find. Adam has settled on Teddy.

The first time he realized he could trust Teddy was outside Counter Culture on a grey Sunday about three months ago. A few of them were there, with nowhere else to go and not enough cash to keep sitting in the café, and Brianna Vicci was trying out her debate thing on Adam. Everyone says her parents pay for a tutor to get her into college, and even though she denies it she has exactly that type of facade, a few smart words that circle back on themselves if challenged. Adam had been reading a book that teaches, among other things, how to win arguments against people like that, how to use their own words against them and beat their smugness into the ground. Brianna's point was pretty basic, just parroting some cable news thing about political engagement, Adam being the only one of them who was old enough to vote. She was drawing a line—a line in crayon—between the fact he hadn't voted and his Cthulhu T-shirt. She even used the word cartoon, which is probably what set Adam off. Adam is strong enough to admit he lost control a little, something the book warns against. He tried the technique where you keep your voice quiet and calm but you say something violent, tone–content disparity it's called, designed to disorient the other person. The idea is that a gentle and reasonable delivery takes an insult or threat outside the accepted conventions of argument, which are all about deception anyway. The move is impossible to respond to, the book says, because it mocks the perceived rules of engagement, gets into the space between irony and earnestness, and forces your opponent to acknowledge that what they're doing is just as contradictory. An emperor's new clothes situation, basically. But you have to go all in or it comes across childish, like you're just being silly. After some harmless back and forth, Adam decided to calmly tell Brianna he could strangle her and bury her body somewhere her family would never find it. There were the expected gasps; Ceecee said he couldn't say things like that. Freya said, Let's just go, let's get the hell away from him. If they had walked away, Adam would have lost. But, as the book promised, enough of them wanted to know what he would say next. If a person receives a shock, they will always want another to confirm the first. That, the book says, is called the invitation to push. Your victim will ask you for more. Adam tried to put a smile into his eyes but not his mouth and went on: They'd visit me in whatever cell I was in, and they'd beg me to tell them where you were. Because they'd want to have a proper funeral, a place they could leave flowers and such. So do you think it would make any difference, Brianna, them knowing where your body was? Because you'd still be dead, right? I'm just asking what you think. Brianna had tightened her shoulders into a tense shrug, and for a moment the breeze in her hair made it seem like Adam's words were literally blowing her backwards. Now he had arrived, he had done his own circling around her. Teddy laughed uncertainly, wanting it to be funny; everyone else was shocked silent. Adam left a suitable pause during which all of them—Brianna, Ceecee, Teddy, and Freya—were focused on him and him alone, and then he went and fucked up the dismount. The book says one of the worst things you can do is swear; it undermines your tone, brings things back in line with the conventions of passionate argument, and, worst of all, makes it seem like you *care*. But Adam was too excited. He was winning. He told Brianna that when her family begged him he would laugh in their fucking faces. He felt the word's anger as he was saying it. It told everyone listening that she had upset him. That was enough to let her back in. He hadn't disoriented her as the book promised. She didn't seem shocked or hurt. Her shoulders dropped and she stepped toward Ceecee and reached for her. Brianna's face and neck were red, but she sounded calmer than Adam when she told him, over and over, that he needed help. She had nothing else to say, no argument, they were past that. She just said the same thing over and over again, the repetition magically changing its meaning each time, the syllables dissolving into noise then reforming as words again. *You need help. You need help, man. You're troubled. You need help.* Adam felt heat flow into his own face. There were ambient sounds of agreement from the others; a bus drove past them, its vibrations moving through the sidewalk and into Adam's legs. Brianna still looked tense, but she clearly wasn't what he wanted her to be. He needed help. He needed help, man. How could she be beating him with just that one line? That's when Teddy stepped in and neutralized everything. It was incredible, like the speech Julius Caesar gave. No, not Caesar, the other guy. Teddy asked Brianna what she knew about non-engagement as a political strategy, if she'd thought through the consequences of lesser-of-two-evils thinking, whether she actually knew who Lovecraft was, and, finally, who she would have voted for, and why. Even Brianna must have known that that last question was unbeatable because all possible answers would be wrong. Teddy used the same tone Adam had, only his substance was reasonable too. Of course everyone jumped on board, wanting to get away from whatever the conversation had become, and soon they were speculating about which parties supported the war.

Usually that kind of embarrassment made Adam want to go off on his own and drink, but because of Teddy he was somehow able to laugh it off. After the girls went home, he and Teddy drove down to the river and talked until it was dark. You know what we should do, Adam said through the music. We should get the fuck out of here. Teddy replied that he had been thinking about going camping in the summer. I don't mean that, Adam said, I mean really get gone. Properly clear. What do you mean *clear*, Teddy asked, then before Adam could answer made a joke of it, putting his fists toward Adam's chest like a defibrillator. Adam slapped the hands away but laughed. He didn't know exactly what he meant, but he told Teddy to imagine driving out of town and knowing they weren't coming back. Where would you go, though, Teddy wondered aloud, opening the truck door either to go piss or to fetch the final two beers that were cooling in the shallows. When he came back it was obvious he had been thinking about it. You mean for the whole summer, he asked. Adam wanted more than just the summer. He wanted to vanish. He wondered if you could drive all the way to the Arctic. They could get work in one of the mines up there. He had seen a video posted by a lawyer who had quit her job and was making double driving a hauler at a copper mine. She got two weeks off out of every four. So why not him? But all he said to Teddy was, At *least* the whole summer. Their cans clicked open and collided with embarrassed affection. There was a slight taste of river slime on the rim, which Adam wiped with his Cthulhu T-shirt. I'm up for it, Teddy said, checking his phone. Yeah, let's get the fuck. For some reason Teddy always says it like that, just *get the fuck*, without the *out of here*. Adam has started saying it that way too.

THIS GAME THEY are playing is one they outgrew years ago. So why play it? For the joke of it, the fact that neither of them needs or wants to win. Teddy on his bed, the controller slick in his palms, Adam on the floor, out of sight except hair and neck. They race laps, smiting each other when they get the chance, swearing fondly, swearing revenge. After so many years of this, Teddy's fingers work of their own accord. The musical motif that means *final lap* is burned into his brain. It will come to him at odd times, like when he hears the front door, the keys in the dish that mean his mother is home. Cue the dramatic flourish while he waits to hear if his parents will speak to each other, or if she will come up the stairs and into his room to tell him everything has changed. Often Teddy feels he is in both places at once, the before and after, which cancel each other out, leaving him nowhere. He wants what will happen to hurry up and happen. He has won the race, incidentally. His avatar begins an automatic victory lap and Adam groans, a pleasant boredom filling the room as they abandon their controllers. They are not drinking: Adam wants to stockpile for the trip. They let the game's plastic music run its loop and they lie there, not looking at each other, friends.

That's when Teddy makes the mistake of suggesting they drive south, across the border. No way, Adam says with surprising force, We're going north. As though he has been waiting for the chance, he starts telling Teddy about failed states, about unsustainable multiculturalism, whatever that might be. When Adam talks like this, Teddy feels excited and uneasy in equal measure, like watching somebody do tricks with a knife. It is not a question of whether he agrees with Adam; he is not asked for his opinion. All he has to do is cling on for the ride, trusting he will end up somewhere he never expected. When he does say something, it is mainly to avoid the appearance of being lectured to, being taught. This country's the same though, he ventures, and is about to mention Indigenous folks, but Adam is not ready to yield. You know about the sixty-percent rule? asks Adam. The sixty-percent *threshold*, he adds, remembering the proper word. That was a slip: now Teddy knows Adam is just repeating something said by one of the bearded guys he subscribes to. Teddy knows where Adam gets this stuff from, but it's still a let-down when you catch out a conjuror. I've heard of it, lies Teddy, who knows he is about to be told anyway. Adam goes on: It's when a society has no dominant culture anymore. If the biggest ethnic group is less than sixty percent of the total, bad things start happening—and guess where America is right now. Teddy nods and says nothing, as though this were all common knowledge. He remembers Adam telling him his mother lived in the States, but doesn't say so. Nor does he tell Adam that he himself might not be white, not properly. One of his grandparents, whom he never met, came from a country Teddy knows next to nothing about.

When it is finally his turn to speak again, he says, It's weird how whiteness is the thing that goes away when you mix races, like Black people can be three-quarters white and they're still like— Exactly right, Adam interrupts, and you want to know why? For them it's a *culture*. But we've decided we're not allowed to do that anymore. Teddy is vaguely aware of his fingers raking his scalp. I can't wait to get out of here, he says. Fun and games, Adam says. Teddy imagines the two of them arriving in a place where they were each the other's only family. He imagines a secret camping spot only the two of them know about, the map he will draw to document its location. By the end of summer he could be a different person. Ceecee won't know him, and he may even be able to tell himself he has outgrown her. He will be ready for whatever comes. So we head north, sounds good, Teddy says. Adam has turned and is looking up at him from the floor. What are you grinning about? he asks. Nothing, Teddy says. I'm just saying it's a good plan.

THEY TELL TEDDY's parents they're going away for a few days or maybe a week, though they've begun to joke to each other that they won't ever come back. Adam thinks about the Arctic coast, the idea of having gone as far as anyone can go. Even if they stood shivering by the sea for five minutes then turned around and drove straight back . . . Or maybe he can put Teddy on a bus home and stay there, be the man to make a life at life's edge. Teddy would be Adam's emissary then, would break the news to his father. He could make Teddy swear not to reveal exactly where he was. Not that Michael was likely to bother looking for him.

Together they fish Teddy's family's camping stuff from the dusty chaos at the back of the garage. Teddy's dad tells Adam to stop regularly and rest. Microsleeps are a real thing, apparently. Your brain can switch off for a moment, just long enough to slam you into a tree or a happy family in the oncoming lane. You don't want to wind up a cautionary tale. That's when Elizabeth says, If you're going to camp, Ted, you should get something for bears. His dad goes upstairs, and when he comes back they're already outside, loading up. Grace has come out onto the porch but doesn't wave, just stares at Adam as he gets into the truck. Teddy's dad jogs over and Adam assumes he's about to hug his son, but instead he opens his palm and inside is cash; Adam can't tell how much.

They drive down Victoria Parade, past the school from which they would otherwise graduate next year, turn into Oakwood Drive, and ten minutes later they cross the jumping bridge. Adam says they'll just head north and see what happens. If there is no plan, it cannot fail. The Arctic would only hang around their necks this early on, or worse, make Teddy laugh. It's true Adam can't quite imagine making it that far. But while Teddy was packing his backpack, Adam checked on his phone and it's only a fifty-hour drive. Maybe we'll end up getting work somewhere along the way, he says. Work, Teddy groans, as if the whole point of the trip were to escape that. Why else had Adam quit McDonald's? We should do something, though, Adam says. When he looks over, Teddy is staring dumbly at his phone, like he's watching the signal bars slip away. What did you tell Cee-cee? asks Adam. Teddy says, Nothing. We don't even know how long we'll be away. Might only be a few nights. She probably won't even notice I'm gone. What did you tell your dad? That sounds weird to Adam, like Teddy has a girlfriend and Adam just has his father. But it gives him the chance to tell Teddy that he hasn't told Michael anything, either, that his dad is going to get home tonight and wonder where he is. Then at some point he'll figure out that all the canned food is gone. Teddy laughs nervously. Fun and games, Adam says. What if he freaks out and reports you missing? asks Teddy. Adam shrugs, the smile thick in his cheeks. I'll message him once we know what the plan is, he says.

In the next town, they pass the marine supply store where Michael is working this very moment. Adam looks over, wanting to farewell the shitty hatchback in the store's parking lot, but he can't see it. At a red light, Adam revs the engine out of joy or relief. It competes, no, harmonizes with the music playing through the stereo from Teddy's phone. A man crossing the street gives Adam a look, and it doesn't bother Adam in the slightest. None of this is real, he thinks. It's all just tendrils that lace themselves around you unless you swat them away, tendrils inching toward your throat. But there is nothing that says the condition has to be permanent. He wishes now he'd brought the book with him: he still has two chapters to go. He pictures the road ahead and decides this will be the last traffic signal he'll have to wait at. But once they're moving again, Teddy turns the music down and says, We have to make a stop. That annoys Adam, the forthrightness of it. Teddy is the passenger. You need to kiss Ceecee goodbye? says Adam. Teddy punches him in the thigh. Pretty hard, actually. It will leave a bruise, even though Adam has said stuff like that before and they've both laughed. As the days run on the bruise will darken, it will turn yellow around a shining purple core. It will fade and fade and disappear. We have to stop, Teddy says, putting a stress on every word like he's the boss suddenly, because I'm going to buy us a rifle.

*

When the man in the polo shirt with the green name badge asks Adam if he's looking for anything in particular, Adam shakes his head, embarrassed. Teddy's arms are folded; he walks along a wall stacked with grey and black metal. The man must sense their diffidence because he goes on talking, telling them what's popular, that the semi-automatics are to the left, to let him know if they have questions. Adam has been doing his best to keep his balance on this new wave. Teddy never told him he had a licence. He says he got it when he was fifteen, for a hunting trip with his dad that never happened. Adam had to laugh when Teddy showed him the card. The photo is of a kid in flannel, grinning like an idiot, a little moustache on the lip he has not yet begun to shave.

Adam has never thought much about hunting. He has no desire to do whatever it is you have to do after you kill the animal. Games are better: the skill and the thrill without the hassle. But now that they are actually in the store, and Teddy is touching various display models, Adam is envious. His father has his licence, too, he remembers, from years back, though there has never been a gun in the house since Adam's been around. Probably a good thing given how depressed Michael is.

The store employee has turned his attention to Teddy, who at least knows enough to ask questions without making an idiot of himself. Adam hangs back, away from the looming wall. A banner above them reads: *The Sportsman's Choice*. The guy shows Teddy an SKS something and a Ruger carbine. Adam knows from Patriot that carbine means a shorter barrel. When Teddy asks about ammunition, Adam wanders away so he won't feel like anyone's kid brother. He decides he'll pay Teddy for half of whatever it costs, but they'll have to sort that out later. It's probably not smart to hand over cash in the store—it's probably the kind of thing they're supposed to report. He browses fishing rods and tackle, knives, tents. They already have Teddy's parents' camp stove. He decides on two plastic canisters, red for gas and blue for water, which will come in handy when towns start to thin out. He picks up a can of bug spray, pleased with himself for having thought of it, and a silver tarpaulin, which just seems like a good thing to have.

Teddy has chosen. It's $349, which must be double the wad his dad gave him, plus more for ammo. I'm good for half, Adam says quietly while the guy rings up the sale and hands a form and a pen to Teddy, but Teddy ignores him or pretends not to hear. The woman at the next register notices Adam standing with his hands full and calls him over. Let me take care of that for you, she says kindly, lifting the awkward canisters from his arms. Among the impulse buys are rolls of black duct tape and pairs of cheap black sunglasses. They match Teddy's new rifle. Adam buys one of each.

On the security footage, it looks like they're both laughing as they walk out of the store, Adam more so than Teddy, who carries the long box under one arm, a plastic bag in his other hand. Adam swings the red canister in a way that makes it obvious it's empty. He is already wearing his new sunglasses, though probably he has only put them on as a joke, or to model them for his friend, because the label is still attached, a little cardboard diamond hanging from the bridge and butting against his nose as the two boys walk beneath the camera and out of frame.

THE ROAD, THOUGH! Endless becoming, a colour palette always and somehow never changing, grey to green to brown to blue to other, occasionally red, very occasionally yellow, whoosh, repeat, repeat, something comes the other way with headlights on, the beauty of headlights in daylight, fence, field, these lane markings like perforations maybe, as if the road or the whole world could unzip any moment now, if there were such a thing as a moment when you're driving, which Teddy realizes there isn't. It's just one long stretch. The road and its contradictions: boredom and excitement, you sit still but you're moving, there's a good kind of silence even with the engine noise and the German metal Adam has them listening to. Teddy's mom used to call this sitting and thinking time. But all Teddy wants to think about is how the world keeps rushing toward them then dropping harmlessly into their wake. Adam is a good driver. He speeds often, especially to pass the empty logging trucks that must be on their way back to tree farms farther north. Adam tells Teddy the German metal is political, but it's in fucking German so how can Adam know? The singer's definitely angry, though. Teddy can't decide if Adam's tastes are more adult or more childish than his own. Is what Teddy likes, let's say Arkells, more grown-up or just more boring? Funny that people call things *middle of the road*. That's where they are now, as Adam passes another rig and swings back in before the line of oncoming traffic can snag them. Somebody beeps, and Teddy lets out a hum to match. Wasn't that a bit close, he thinks but doesn't say. He thinks about rhythm and speed, about the fact that they don't know where they're going.

At a gas station they buy energy drinks and for an hour they talk eagerly over the music, looking for ways to express how free they feel. Then comes the crash, spiralling silences in which the music speaks for them and Teddy nearly falls asleep. Towns go by, billboards, fruit trees, fences. The images don't stop when he closes his eyes, and when he opens them again he sees something amazing. Two horses are standing nose to nose in a field, perfectly still, like somebody glued them together. They look like statues or oversized toys. One of them is wearing a halter around its head, the other isn't. Somehow this makes Teddy think of the French they had done at school, how pointless it was because no one could remember anything by the time the next class came around. The recap would take more than half the time, the teacher getting more and more frustrated. But what did she expect? To Adam he says, over the music, Do you remember when you asked that French teacher if the word for cat also meant pussy? Adam laughs, then says, Wait, are you sure that was me? I don't remember that. It was absolutely you, Teddy says. They hadn't been proper friends back then, but he remembers it, his green pencil case, how the boys all laughed and the girls groaned and the teacher just went on as though Adam hadn't said anything. She was telling them about two words that sounded almost the same, and you had to be careful or you'd end up telling somebody about your horses. She was showing off, trying to make the class laugh, but Adam stole her thunder with the pussy comment. Thinking about it now, years later, Teddy decides that Adam's comment was actually pretty smart. It was really about how pointless the whole situation was, how they were all wasting their time, the teacher included.

They're going too fast to have the windows open and the truck's AC is broken. You only need it two weeks of the year anyway, Adam jokes. But surely these will be those weeks. It's late afternoon and the sun is still well above the trees. On a long, mild hill the truck seems to struggle until Adam drops a gear. Teddy feels sweat on his neck and in his little pocket of chest hair. Away to the right are miles of quiet forest, places where nobody ever goes, probably full of bugs and bears. He hates himself for not being able to drive.

Stopping is glorious, a chance to move and to fart and to breathe. They both balance on shin-high posts beside a trash can, performing a laughing parody of martial art, for no reason other than the joy of controlling their bodies, of coordinating, synchronizing. Slowly the game becomes a competition, who can jump one-legged from post to post without falling. Knowing their phones will eventually fail them, they buy a map and unfurl it on the truck's hood, captain and first mate. They can go anywhere they want. Teddy plants a finger at the tiny pink words HOT SPRINGS, feeling the engine's heat through the waxy paper. Adam steers them north and east, away from the coast where they spent their boyhoods. Inward, toward what comes next. As the sun finally hits the treetops, Teddy tears open a softened chocolate block and passes it to Adam by the row. It leaves sweet muck on their hands, and later, as he stares out the window into the dusk, Teddy realizes he is sucking his thumb. The more the light goes, the more it is his own face he sees in the glass, lit by the blue stereo glow, already a ghost.

Each town they pass through is smaller than the last, recognizable brands slowing to a trickle. They stop for the night on the outskirts of one place, at a bend in the river that looks deserted enough. Adam says they're far enough from the town that no one will bother them but close enough that they can walk back to that bar they passed. They'd probably get served in a town that small. He parks beside a low track that runs into a sea of pebbles and what looks like a ford through the black water. Teddy can imagine it flooding. Even with the driving done he remains a passenger, watching as Adam unfolds the tarpaulin and ties its ends to the truck's raised trunk. There's only one good tree, so Adam squats by the river and lets the water fill one of his new canisters. Then he lugs it back to use as an anchor. Teddy is impressed, and determined to make his own contributions. He doesn't want to end up with the domestic jobs while Adam does the fun stuff, but with no other options he gets the camp stove out of its mesh sack and tries to remember how the pieces slot together. The burner hisses when he finally lights it, a memory of childhood, of hunger and the happiness of being somewhere other than home. This, he thinks, will be the summer his mother finally leaves his father and goes off with Ron; maybe he will arrive back to find everything dealt with, like how he avoids the kitchen until he knows the dishes are done. He hears the click of a bourbon bottle opening for the first time. Adam has scored three from his cousin, Teddy doesn't know on what terms. Fuck, Teddy says. We don't have a can opener. Yeah we do, Adam says, handing him his utility knife. Teddy repeatedly pushes its hook through the metal lid, making notch after notch until he has torn a jagged mouth. Probably he did it wrong, but Adam doesn't say anything.

They sit with scalding cans between their knees, two mouths making plenty of noise. In brief moments of quiet Teddy hears other things, birds crying in the dark and the persistent river. They pass the bourbon back and forth, and Teddy is happy. He is part of a team. You think we can make it to the Arctic? asks Adam. You mean the ocean? Yeah, Adam says. Jesus, Teddy says, how far is that? Adam's voice is defensive. It doesn't take that long, maybe a week. A week there and a week back, Teddy says doubtfully. He doesn't mention how much it would cost in gas because then Adam would try to buy half the rifle off him again, which would defeat the purpose of having it. Plus he wonders what happens if they get bored, have a fight, or just get sick of each other. He leans back and looks at the stars beyond the tarp, telling himself to relax and enjoy the ride. It's a lot of driving to do on your own, he says eventually. Maybe, Adam says, not taking the bait. Adam suggests again that they walk to the bar, but this time it sounds more hypothetical. Both of them have taken root in their camping chairs, staring like old men at the darkness that must be the river. By the time the bourbon is a quarter gone, they're both half-asleep. They lay their mats and sleeping bags side by side in what Adam calls the camper, a rigid bubble bolted to the rear part of the truck. When Teddy closes his eyes he sees the blue flame from the camp stove, then the blue light from the car stereo, then the horses. How weird they looked, how fake, but they were definitely real.

Teddy wakes first. He shimmies outside, clicking the tailgate closed so as not to rouse Adam, enjoying the sense of having the morning to himself. He walks barefoot through the dirt, locates his boots, puts the same socks back on. This river isn't like the one in their town: it's darker and more muscular, deeper too. He leans on the cold hood and looks at blistered beer cans and blackened rocks, the ashes of whomever camped here last. Sheep or maybe goats bleat from somewhere across the river, and Teddy smiles to himself. There is something reassuring about this place, the opposite of the country tourists come to see. No soaring firs or mountains or jewel-coloured lakes, just a trashed-up gravel track beside murky water, the tangled shrubs on the opposite bank dipping their lowest branches into the current.

He is slightly disappointed when sounds from the truck announce Adam. Teddy sits on one of the camping chairs in what he hopes is a posture of contemplation. The chair was left outside the tarpaulin's shadow, though, and dew begins to soak into his jeans. When Adam emerges he is still in his underwear; without saying anything he walks to the river and pisses right into the current, an arc and a splash. Gross, Teddy shouts, but he's smiling. Makes no difference, Adam calls back. It all gets to the sea eventually. Besides, how much sheep shit you think is already in that water? We need to get some proper food, Teddy says, like a bag of apples and some bread and some peanut butter. Adam walks back, wiping a hand on his boxers. Unscrewing the cap of yesterday's energy drink, he says, I have to buy a toothbrush too, but first things first. He gives Teddy a look, and Teddy doesn't have to ask what it means. Let's do it, Teddy says, but not here. Let's get away from the town and these farms, find some forest. From behind the shrubs across the river, the animals bleat their agreement.

ADAM HAS BEEN gaming so much he sees the screen when he closes his eyes. Ever since summer vacation began, if he wasn't doing weights, hanging out with Teddy, or on shift at McDonald's, he was on the couch in his room, playing Patriot. He and Teddy meet online sometimes, but Teddy is not exactly an asset; he spends too much time with Ceecee and never takes it seriously anyway. Adam has his others, his in-game friends, strangers he plays and chats with. He's good, too, good enough to be invited to a group chat where a bunch of what seem like older guys talk shit and share links, which is how he first heard about the book. The chat is called Safe Space, which is both a joke and not a joke. Right now, being offline feels cleansing. He wants the game's images to fade and give way to real ones. Otherwise, he will get complacent. Last night he even dreamt in the night-visiony green of a mission. Nothing happened in the dream, he was just walking dully along, the tip of his weapon arcing back and forth the way it does in first-person POV. Being on the road with Teddy makes him feel calmer, not so constantly pent up like when he's bored at home and school. He hasn't even felt like jerking off. Sometimes he'll get an urge just from something in the game, like crawling commando toward an enemy in darkness or aiming at the back of some oblivious herder's turbaned head. Who knows why. It's not as though the thought of killing turns him on, it isn't that, it's more like crossed wires in his brain, one feeling reminding him of the other. Maybe it's about having power over somebody, like what the guys in porn must feel when the girl goes crazy. One of his Patriot friends joked that you play better if you haven't come for a while, that the aggression helps. But why should we have been made that way, Adam wonders, with morality crusted on top like a hasty paint job, and the truth seething below? Maybe it's just him, maybe he's a freak like everyone says. It isn't the sort of thing he can talk about, to Teddy or anyone else. Anyway, Teddy is different because he's fucking now, which is probably the way out of the conundrum, but it's also a whole other trap. So much focus has been on the hazards of sex for women, and rightly so, that nobody, until now, has talked about what dangers it holds for men. He learned that from a streamer he follows, a guy who monologues while he plays and whose thinking seems sharpened by the mechanics of combat. There is something potent about hearing a persuasive talker discuss politics while watching his avatar progress relentlessly through the game world, killing whomever needs killing, operating with strength and skill and grace. The voice and the figure in fatigues are on completely different planes, yet they complement and enhance each other. Something in Adam understands that he must bring mind and body together in the real world, away from the safe space of Patriot, without phone reception, without even the book, which he decided at the last moment not to bring.

He had hesitated when throwing things into his backpack: to let Teddy read it would be to let the curtain drop, to admit that a lot of what Adam says is not his own thinking at all, just stuff he has lifted from some smarter, older guy. On the other hand it calmed him, helped him feel in control of himself. In the end it stayed behind along with the forgotten toothbrush, and Adam wonders now what he'll do with Teddy there all the time, with only the camper to sleep in and nowhere to be alone except the forest and gas station restrooms. It's not as though he won't get the urge eventually. Even the thought of what they're about to do this morning makes him feel something, not turned on, but something. He should have dunked himself in that river, sheep shit or no. Teddy said it would be dangerous, that it was moving too fast. It sure looked black.

When they reach the other side of the sad, silent town, Adam drives more carefully. He slows to look down smaller roads and turnouts. They choose one that winds away uphill. It's paved, or was, but it's clear nobody uses it anymore. Adam drums the wheel between each turn. Over the hill the road gets even worse, with ruts and even saplings piercing the cracked asphalt. He pulls to the side and turns the engine off. For a moment he and Teddy both sit there, listening, as if to make sure they're alone. There are great walls of firs on either side of them, a carpet of needles giving the hillside gentle curves, like brown snow. Adam climbs out of the cab.

In the camper he takes a mouthful of energy drink and gets new underwear from his backpack. He is halfway through changing when Teddy opens up the back. Adam feels the cold air on his skin even before either of them says anything. Oh, sorry man, says Teddy, but he doesn't leave until he's taken the boxed rifle and the ammo from beneath the folded tarpaulin. Then, as he turns away, Teddy says, Let's head up the hill a bit. Adam finishes dressing and grabs last night's spaghetti can to aim at, then changes his mind and throws it back into the truck. Surely they can find something better.

Teddy is already among the trees; Adam will have to jog to catch up. He didn't put socks on, and his toes are beginning to slime up in his boots. They will have to wash today, or start to smell. The way Teddy holds the rifle reminds Adam of his dream. When he reaches Teddy's position, they walk in silence between the trunks. It's not quiet—there are loads of birds making a racket. He can't remember the last time he heard so many. I thought the woods were supposed to be peaceful, he jokes. I guess we're not usually awake this early, Teddy says. One of the birds has a call like a cartoon whip. Another is growlier, almost human. Let's shoot them, Adam says, and Teddy seems game. They stop and stare into the trees, but neither of them can actually see the birds. We're being too loud, Teddy says, an accusation. The firs have given way to something else, trunks that feel rough and good against Adam's hands. When he looks up he sees warping snatches of sky between swaying crowns. He stops a minute and stares upwards, gets dizzy from it. Each treetop seems to reach for its neighbour then pull back just before it makes contact. He doesn't know what kind of trees they are, but he decides he likes them. Shh, Teddy says, and Adam realizes he has been humming. He feels a little rush of anger at being scolded, but Teddy, after all, is holding a gun, which trumps everything. Teddy squats against a mossy log and loads the rifle. Adam tries to memorize each step, while trying not to seem like he is watching too closely. It makes Teddy look weirdly skilful; he's a different person with the rifle against his chest. He even walks differently, with shoulders forward, a posture Adam recognizes from gaming and wants to make fun of, but they've agreed to be silent now. Teddy stops beside a thick trunk and says something very softly, just a breath. Adam reaches Teddy's shoulder and looks past him at a creamy blur, an animal obscured by the trees. It's maybe fifty metres away. A snowshoe. In fact, two of them. One is doing its undulating little hop, the other is stock still, ears erect. Teddy slowly raises the rifle to his shoulder, and Adam instinctively steps back. But they're a long way off. Surely Teddy has to get closer. Adam wants to tell him but knows better than to make a sound. He has never seen anything die in real life. He hit a cat in the truck the first week he had it but didn't stick around to see what happened. He can feel his heart as he watches Teddy's shoulder and arm tense. Teddy's hand is obscuring the trigger, meaning Adam doesn't know when the shot will come. He waits for it, looking from the distant hares to the black barrel to his friend's greasy hair. Teddy only started shaving last year and doesn't get proper stubble like Adam does. The gun somehow makes him look even younger, Adam decides; it's like watching a kid riding a too-big bike. For a moment, one of the animals is more clearly visible, its ridiculous ears sticking up like a dare. It's oblivious, thinks Adam, it's ignorant. These things do not equate to innocence in his mind. A rod for the fool's back.

The shot makes him step back and bring his hands toward his ears, but he catches himself and drops them to his sides again. He will have to get used to that. He remembers rather than hears the little chime as the casing hits something, as the hares get magically swallowed by the shrubs. He is still trying to find himself, but Teddy has already lowered the gun and is walking toward the place. Adam follows dumbly, a few paces behind. When Teddy reaches the spot, he leans the rifle on a tree and kneels, pretending to be some expert tracker, the gun just propped beside him. Adam could easily pick it up himself, but doesn't. He stands there, reverberating. No blood, Teddy says softly. Adam, coming back to himself, says: Sniper level zero. Teddy laughs and says, Come on, they were too far away. He stands, picks up the rifle, aims, and shoots again, either at a bird or at nothing. Then he turns and offers the weapon to Adam. You want a go? Teddy says it the way boys have always said it, right back to the earliest sharing of toys, with pride and reluctance. There's a harmony to the gun's weight, the way it pulls at Adam's arms, asking his muscles to do the tiniest amount of work. Suddenly the way his toes slide inside his boots feels pleasant instead of gross, and he no longer wants to shower or eat or take a shit. He lets Teddy instruct him. He picks a spot, adjusts his posture. Don't forget the safety's still on, Teddy says respectfully. Adam lowers and clicks it off. Always use safety but never rely on safety, Teddy recites. I remember that from the course I did. We all had to— Adam shoots over his words. The stock jabs his shoulder, not as hard as he had expected. He hears the bullet whistle away. He swings as he aims again, looking for something specific, wanting to make more sound before Teddy has the chance to say anything else. More rabbits, please. Teddy moves as Adam does, always staying behind his shoulder. It's all so much slower than it is in Patriot. It would be impossible if the target were moving, and yet so many men are experts at this. Because they practise, Adam tells himself. It's like anything else. Teddy tells him to straighten a little, to bring the stock higher, to keep both eyes open. But there is nothing to aim at; it has all been scared away. Teddy takes hold of Adam's shoulders and shapes him, saying, Try to hit that tree, the paler one dead ahead. Adam lowers the gun. No point, he says, shrugging Teddy's hands off him. Let's wait until there's something worth shooting—we've got a long way to go. But Adam does keep hold of the rifle as they descend the hill, carrying it the way his avatar does, right hand curled beneath its centre of mass so he doesn't even have to grip but just lets it balance in his sweaty palm. The birds are singing again, but more quietly now, cautiously.

TOWARD DUSK, WHEN Adam says he's tired, Teddy offers to drive. This is a gambit, because of course Teddy cannot drive, especially not the truck, which isn't even an automatic. But it seems only fair after teaching Adam how to load the rifle. Teddy could not explain why he hasn't learned until now, except that the longer he put it off the harder it was to ask for help. A while back, even his sister offered to teach him, and he surprised himself with how aggressively he rejected her. With Adam it will be different. And it will be different here, he thinks, on this vacant, gentle road that shows no sign of ever reaching a junction. He imagines surprising everyone back home by passing his test without seeming to have practised, then borrowing the car on weekends like Grace does. He imagines going over to Adam's house to pick *him* up.

Adam doesn't exactly shoot down Teddy's offer but doesn't say yes either. He says it's time to find a place to camp, anyway, before it gets too dark and they can't see what they're doing. He slaps a thigh and adds, Let's crack that bourbon, I could do with a drink. Sounds good to me, Teddy replies, lifting his butt off the seat to let the blood back in. Adam goes on, fatherishly:

49

A good drink after a day's work. Teddy doesn't know what work either of them has done, but he agrees anyway. He looks at his phone, but there's no signal. A good thing they bought that map or they would be flying blind. Suddenly, Adam turns the music down almost to nothing and says, What did you tell her? Who? says Teddy. Don't play dumb, Adam says, and they both laugh. Teddy looks at the phone screen and his voice gets slightly higher as he talks: I just told her we were going away. Yeah, but did you make it sound like it was just a few days or what? asks Adam. Teddy sighs and looks out his window. There is a low metal guardrail skimming alongside them. Its height fluctuates, as though different sections have been replaced at different times, and finally it descends to the earth and disappears. Beyond the roadside blur are the darker, slower treetops. The sky is pretty, like fruit. They've been following this river for as long as Teddy can remember, the water slowly colouring in the failing sun. It doesn't seem to be getting any wider or narrower; it just snakes its fat curves toward the road and then away, toward the road and then away. Did you tell her it was just a road trip? asks Adam, insistent. I just said we were going, Teddy says. What else would I have said? We don't even know what we're doing, or how long for. There is the faintest hint of complaint in Teddy's voice, which feels like a mistake. Message her again, says Adam, taking one hand off the wheel to rub his leg. Tell her we're never coming back. It'll freak her out. The truck speeds up to overtake a white camper van, and Teddy finds himself typing, *Adam says to say we're not coming back.* There's no signal, so who cares. But once he hits send, it will send automatically the next time they're in range. It will sound like a joke or, better, like Adam's starting to piss him off, like he'd rather be on this trip with her. It will make Teddy seem helpless in the passenger seat, a hostage even. They cross a low bridge and its railings make a pulsing sound even through rolled-up windows. What did you write? asks Adam. Teddy looks up at the road and says: That we're not coming back. Adam smiles, rubs his leg again. Once we get off this highway you can start doing some driving, he says. As long as you're careful. That way we can go farther in a day. Sounds good, Teddy says, trying not to sound as excited or as nervous as he feels. He lets the phone clatter audibly into the plastic door pocket and puts his socked feet on the dash. They must have turned west because late sun is pouring through the windshield now. His parents and Grace will be sitting on three sides of the dinner table. Or maybe his mom will be out with Ron. That's been happening more often lately, his dad in the kitchen with that idiot smile, saying, I guess it's just us tonight, kids, as though all three of them didn't know what was going on. Grace will be gone to college soon and it will just be him and his dad at the table, like it is at Adam's house. By now Adam's dad will have noticed that his son is gone. Teddy doesn't know whether to be impressed or worried that Adam left without saying anything. Maybe Ceecee and Brianna are right about Adam being crazy. Maybe Ceecee will use Teddy's taking off as an excuse to break up with him via text. He's petrified of that happening, but at the same time he longs for it in a way he cannot yet articulate, and this is partly why he is here in Adam's truck, letting himself be driven into the interior. He flicks a crumb from his thigh and tries to loosen the seat belt from his shoulder. He can feel the ick of old candy on his tongue. He cups his mouth and breathes himself back in. You still didn't get a toothbrush, he says to Adam. Pass me my sunglasses, Adam says. Teddy hands them over and gets a Thanks, man. Tomorrow they will have been together for two whole days, the longest he can remember being with anyone who wasn't family, even Ceecee.

A little before dark they find a turnout. Adam unfolds the tarpaulin and rigs his silver canopy again. They piss, drink bourbon, eat a family bag of ketchup-flavoured chips, piss again, then crawl into their sleeping bags. Tonight they keep their backpacks between them when they sleep, a tacit gesture toward giving each other the tiniest bit of privacy. I want to drive until we run out of road, Adam says through the dark. I don't see why we can't make the northern coast. When Teddy says nothing, Adam adds, If we share the driving. Teddy yawns and says, It'd be sweet to see it. Maybe let's go by those hot springs and then see how we feel. Always the voice of reason, says Adam.

In the morning Teddy feels sick, stomach unsettled and shit sloppy, but he knows better than to complain. He realizes he's been assuming they'd get bored and turn back by the end of the week, once they started to feel dirty and miss proper food or had spent all their money in roadside places. But that seems less likely now. Adam seems to have a plan. Probably what he's going to do is test Teddy, see how far he'll go before asking to be taken home. Then Adam will be able to say Teddy ruined the adventure by being a pussy. In the meantime, Teddy can at least get some driving under his belt. He wonders if he could convince his parents to buy him and Grace a car. Then Grace would move to college and the car would be his by default. The daydream, and getting back on the road, ease his stomach. The next time he looks at his phone he sees that yesterday's messages have sent, even though they never passed through a town or anything. Ceecee's response has come too: two question marks. That's all, and now they're out of range again. So she's mad. Teddy is relieved enough to decide he misses her. And he is happy to have her to miss. It makes the trip feel more meaningful. When Teddy thinks of Ceecee, he thinks mainly of her body, but he also likes the way she makes fun of him when there's nobody else around, when it's just them. He likes the way she tries to pull his arms more tightly around her. Sometimes she is too much for him. A few weeks ago she wanted him to lick her eyeball, said someone had told her it felt nice. Jesus. Was that what being adventurous meant? He went irredeemably limp, slipped out of her like a turd. Then she refused to do it to him, even when he offered his face to her, pulling his eyelid wide like in that movie. They'd ended up laughing about it and she got him hard again, but he still felt like he'd failed something. All of these tests wear him down. He has read that at least half of girls are faking at least half the time, which are not great odds. There's always a moment afterwards when he wants to ask, but it would make him seem even more clumsy than he already feels. Plus he's frightened she'll confirm what he suspects. Last night, lying beside Adam in the dark, he felt like looking at the pictures he has of her. But phone glow would

53

have given him away, and he'd never have heard the end of it if Adam had guessed what he was doing.

NOW EASE OUT until you feel it bite—but slowly. Adam is in the passenger seat. He can feel wetness on his lower back, his upper lip. In his belly button. The back of his neck stings. A pattern of heat swims across the dash. What do you mean *bite*? says Teddy. You know, Adam says patiently, that feeling when it engages. Just let the pedal out slowly and it'll tense up, and that's when you press the gas. But nothing's happening, Teddy says, and I think it's all the way out. Adam glances at the gear stick and at Teddy's straining face. He looks like he's trying to take a shit. It can't be, Adam says, and as he says that the truck lurches and stalls. Fuck, Teddy says, beating his thighs with both hands. Honestly, fuck it. How come you make it look so easy? Adam tries to laugh but he's too sticky, too uncomfortable and hot. There's no air. Before, when they had the windows open, the truck filled with midges and they spent the next five minutes slapping themselves. All the bug spray seemed to do was burn his skin. It *is* easy, Adam says, once you've done it a thousand times. Teddy doesn't answer, just stares at the windshield, arms folded like he's refusing the steering wheel's advances. Adam can't work out why Teddy is getting so upset about it. Did he really think he'd master a clutch in two minutes? C'mon, Adam says, elbowing Teddy in an encouraging way, try it again. Teddy sighs and puts his hands back on the wheel. But he doesn't start the engine. He stares toward where the track curves away out of sight, where the arrow-straight fir trunks kiss the roadside. Adam coaxes: If we both drive, we can go twice as far. We can do shifts—one drives and the other one sleeps. Twice as far *where?* says Teddy, still staring through the windshield. That's the point, Adam says. Wherever we want.

When Teddy finally gets them going, they move farther up the track, grinding along in a gear too low. Adam keeps telling him to change up, but Teddy's knuckles are white on the wheel and he just guns the accelerator to the point where Adam worries he'll do damage. The truck makes a great animal roar when Teddy puts the clutch in without dropping off the revs, and even then he doesn't change up, just releases the pedal and they gum back into second-gear speed. For shit's sake, Teddy, Adam says above the noise. He is losing patience. Then, for some reason, Teddy finally shifts to third while halfway up a hill, falters, and stalls again. He flicks the ignition roughly off and then on, firing the starter with his foot nowhere near the clutch. Fucksake—be careful, Adam shouts, as instinctively his own left foot jerks onto an imagined pedal. We have to open the windows, Teddy says, I can't breathe. And even though that's exactly what Adam was thinking, he says, We only just got rid of all those bugs. I don't care, Teddy says, it's boiling in here. Adam puts more bug spray on his hands and his ears as Teddy rolls down the driver's side window. The worst is the noise they make when they get close, how cheerful they sound, like they're fucking with him, trying to trick him into slapping his own head.

A couple of hours later Adam is behind the wheel again, taking them down an unpaved track away from the main road. It's slow going, snaking back and forth to avoid the worst of the potholes and the scrubby little shin-high branches that scratch the doors as they pass. This trip will be the end of his truck. Teddy reaches over and pulls his backpack from behind the seats, unzipping the front pocket and getting out a plain black baseball cap. With his seat belt off Adam is getting bumped around quite a bit, which adds to the anticipation. According to the map, the ruins are on a ridge up ahead. What kind of ruins, they have no idea. But if they take the track until they feel a sharp bend to the left, then walk uphill to the right, they should find out. The map shows three pink shapes where the slope flattens out, two squares and an *L*, and the promising word in pink block letters. Adam imagines a derelict farm, the life sucked out of it but life's remnants still there: crockery, furniture. He might find something, a memento, something to take with him into his new life, his new home. He imagines a cabin at a mine in the Arctic, a space that's all his. He imagines money, and respect.

When he decides they've reached the bend, he pulls off to the right. There's no sign of a trail or anything, no evidence that anyone else has been here. Outside, the sun is fierce on the boys' skin. Teddy adjusts his baseball cap and says, After this I'm going to do a bottle wash. Adam agrees. He needs to clean his junk, his armpits, his ass. He wants to take his backpack in case they find something worth keeping, so he empties it of everything but a bottle of water and a Snickers that's warm and soft as shit. It will have to be sucked from the wrapper. He is about to close the door when he thinks of the rifle in its box beneath the tarp. He takes it out, making sure not to ask Teddy's permission; he has a right to it after what Teddy did to his gearbox earlier. You think we bring? asks Teddy when he sees Adam holding it. In case bears, Adam says. They have both started unconsciously paring their sentences, seeing how minimal they can make them and still be understood. If they stayed together long enough, they would end up with their own language.

It is not easy picking their way up the hillside—the ground is mainly loose shale pierced by clusters of a thorny shrub. Here and there are hollows filled with last year's deciduous leaves. I bet this is the kind of place where forest fires start, Teddy says between breaths. Adam has the gun nestled in one hand, perfectly balanced. The sun is behind them, on their necks, and when Adam looks back he sees that Teddy has turned his baseball cap backwards, a little tongue of hair poking through the hole above the snap. Adam says the word *dude* and does the Hawaiian thing with his free hand. Well enjoy your sunburn, Teddy says. Adam says, Shit, we didn't bring the map, did we. They're both breathing heavily from the climb, enjoying the feeling of power in their legs after sitting so long in the truck. Neither wants to slow the other down, so they're climbing fast, slipping back a little with each step they take over the loose rocks. We won't need it, Teddy says. Once we're on the ridge it'll be obvious.

And anyway, I bet there won't be much to see. They mark stuff like that on the map for hikers to navigate by, not because it's anything worth looking at.

And the ruins, it's true, are a disappointment: a few squat stone walls that have long since fallen or been pushed inwards, the barest remains of a structure. It doesn't look like an Indigenous thing, Teddy says as they circle a knee-high pile of crumbled stone sprouting yellow-flowered weeds. Yeah, no skulls, Adam says. They drift apart, wandering disappointed through crackling grass, each trying to coax a story from the place. Adam feels dirty. The sweat from the climb cools in the breeze and almost makes him shiver.

There is one thing, which Adam calls Teddy over to witness: a largish mouse, lying on its side with claws bunched into tiny fists and a sad little whiskered face. Not long dead. It's not very remarkable except that it's lying smack bang in the middle of a circular piece of stone, like a sacrifice. Cute little guy, Teddy says, turning it over with a twig. Its body is perfectly stiff, its tail curled into a rigid smile. I know, Teddy says finally, maybe something caught it, like an eagle or a hawk or whatever, but then dropped it mid-air. It probably had a heart attack, Adam says. Birds of prey can only detect movement, Teddy goes on, so if they drop something that's dead they can't find it again. It's easier for them to go kill something else. Adam leans close, wondering at the tiny slits of its closed eyes, that something so small could have all the same features that a person has. Teddy flicks the twig and the dead mouse springs into the air, high enough to graze Adam's lips. Adam lurches back, spits. Are you fucking serious? Teddy, laughing, says, I didn't think I'd get you. It's probably diseased, Adam says. At least give me your water bottle to wash my mouth out. Use your own, Teddy says. I don't want you infecting my water. Tough, give it, Adam says, and Teddy does.

They sit for a while in silence on the warm stones, then walk back, arms swinging. Adam feels his body complaining with each step, though he is not looking forward to being back in the driver's seat. They are almost halfway down when he says, Oh shit. What? asks Teddy, and Adam shows him two empty hands. We left the rifle. We, Teddy says pointedly. You were the one who wanted to take it. Jesus, don't cry, Adam says. I just put it down where that rodent was. He digs into his pocket and hands Teddy the keys to the truck.

Back at the top of the ridge Adam collects the rifle from where he left it, beside the dead mouse now lying in the grass. If they were still children, he would take the mouse and put it in Teddy's sleeping bag or something. But there are more sophisticated ways to get even. He can see the truck from here, and Teddy's lower half as he leans into the camper. Adam sits down and slowly inspects the gun, cocking it, practising the steps Teddy taught him. He draws a bead on a bird flying in the distance. Then he stands, chooses a cube of stone in one of the clusters several yards away, and fires. He misses what he was aiming for, but gets another piece of stone, which splinters. The sound is surprisingly similar to what it would be in Patriot; games are getting truer to life. He aims at the dead mouse in the grass and fires again. He walks slowly toward the one intact wall and fires through a hole where a window once was, forcing himself to keep moving through the recoil. Each time the stock hits his shoulder it feels more pleasant, the gun less like a toy, more like a tool. What's even nicer than the sudden violence of each shot is the way a new kind of silence rushes into its wake every time, telling him that something has changed. Adam lowers the rifle and looks at the wide sky, the needle-points of trees below the bald hilltop. Until now, he has not properly looked at the view, the ridge far off beyond the valley where he parked. Behind the truck, the sun is reflecting off what must be a curve of river. It's beautiful, he decides. He feels as though a special gift is allowing him to take everything in at once: sky, trees, his truck, his friend waiting patiently. So he eats his messy Snickers, licks his fingers, and wipes the brown on his pants. Then he tosses the wrapper and stays up there a few minutes more, just looking.

When he gets back to the truck, Teddy is in the passenger seat. He stares at Adam like he's waiting for him to explain the shots and the delay. But Adam doesn't, and Teddy doesn't seem to have the balls to challenge him. I need to wash, Adam says. I did already, Teddy says moodily. Just a bottle wash. You were gone ages. Adam doesn't answer but slides the rifle behind the seats. It's going to be sweet when we get to those springs, he says loudly as he walks to the tailgate. Yeah, Teddy calls back. Adam fills an empty soda bottle from the water canister and undresses. He wets his armpit hair, his junk, ass, and feet, soaps them up with Teddy's shower gel, then rinses it all off with what's left in the bottle.

THE BEST THING about driving north in summer is the sense of an arc, nature slipping from arrogance to grim determination. Day, season, Earth all sharing the same curve, and the trees looking more and more heroic. When Teddy cracks his window the chill burns one ear. High clouds send shadows skipping across the valley, which for most of the morning has been grassy and vast, its river off to the left somewhere, out of sight. He rolls up the window and begins telling Adam that Grace got into a university in the east, that she'll be moving there for the start of semester. Fuck that, Adam says, but he sounds impressed. I don't know, Teddy says. It sounds pretty sweet to me. A good way to get the fuck. He fills the next pause by asking Adam what he wants to do after they graduate. Adam says, I told you, I'm not going back. Ergo, I'm not graduating. Teddy laughs at *ergo*; he knows exactly where Adam learned it. He feels like calling Adam's bluff. So don't go back, he says, nobody's making you.

Outside is endless grass, studded here and there with black bushes. How can he avoid being left behind? They are all on their way somewhere: his friend, his girlfriend, his sister, even his mother. Teddy is not thrilled by the prospect of manhood, but he has not yet settled on an alternative. He is shopping for shortcuts. This is why he is here, and why he first started going to the bridge with Adam. He is clinging to the railing, and sooner or later he will have to open his fists and fall. The truck passes through a brief patch of shadow, somebody flicking a light switch off and on. This is a smaller road than the one before; Teddy can't remember passing another car all day. Out of nowhere, Adam says the last thing he will ever do is get a girl pregnant. Then he starts teasing Teddy, telling him he'll be a daddy soon whether he likes it or not, and then he'll have no choice but to go where the current takes him. Teddy puts his ear against the cold window. Most of the things he can think to say in response would be too cruel, amounting to an escalation he doesn't want. Win by too great a margin and you haven't won at all, just expanded the battle into new fronts. He opts instead for the benign counterattack: What about you then? Where exactly are you planning to escape to? Adam drums the steering wheel hard enough to make the horn croak, then gestures through the windshield. What are you talking about, he says, I'm doing it right now. This is it. But this isn't a place, Teddy says. At some point you've got to arrive somewhere, do something. What are you going to *do*? Adam is silent for a moment then says, I'm going to mine gold. They both laugh; Teddy unscrews the cap from his energy drink. And a minute later, as if he's been rehearsing it in his head, Adam adds: I mean it, I'm not going back. And unless you want to walk, neither are you. Fuck off, Teddy says, because all he can do is act as though Adam is joking, and Adam knows this. When Teddy glances over at his friend's face, he does not want Adam to return the look, does not want those small eyes on him. In this moment Teddy is glad Adam is doing all the driving: it means his eyes are mostly on the road. Teddy remembers the first time Adam took him to jump into the river. They've done it a thousand times by now, but the first time carries weight. Adam vaulted onto the railing like it was nothing. When Teddy got up there they stood side by side, looking down. They both had to touch a hand to each other's shoulder to keep their balance. He remembers Adam looking at him then, those small eyes, pupils tiny in the sun. Teddy was uncomfortable and chose to look down at the water, at the rocky banks closing in on the patch where Adam was assuring him it was safe to jump. Adam adjusted his grip on the stanchion and with his other hand nudged Teddy off balance. Instinctively Teddy stepped forward, only a fraction, to catch his weight, but there was nowhere to step. He can still picture the sight of Adam's face in his peripheral. On the way down he decided he hated Adam, planned to put a knee right through his stomach. Or better yet, to walk up to Adam's truck and take the handbrake off, let it roll right into the river. But once he struck the water and surfaced, he saw that Adam was not up on the bridge, looking down at Teddy and laughing. Adam was right there beside him; he had followed Teddy down without Teddy realizing it. And this made Teddy wonder if he really had been pushed, or if they'd both just stumbled over the edge. Adam made a shrill, joyful noise, and Teddy decided then and there that he had enjoyed the fall.

*

Teddy wakes to Adam punching him lightly on the thigh. He groans a question mark, stretching. He has that eerie feeling that comes from falling asleep in a moving vehicle and waking up to find it stationary, silent. The grassland from earlier has disappeared, and there are now trees on both sides of the road, hemming them in. Adam has pulled onto the shoulder, and just ahead of them on the opposite side is a canary-yellow van with blinking hazards. Two people sit on either side of a pink picnic table. Why'd you stop, Teddy says. He looks at the figures across the road. Their shiny camping bottles glint in the sun. The van's engine is uncovered, but they don't look like people who just broke down in the middle of nowhere. They're waving their arms around like maniacs. Did you stop for those girls? asks Teddy. He yawns. You're still dreaming, man, Adam says. Can't you see the one on the left is a dude? And Adam's right—the guy has even longer hair than the girl. Neither of them seems to have noticed Teddy and Adam. They're playing some kind of game, slamming their hands on the table and laughing. Adam starts the engine and edges forward, rolling down his window at the same time. When they get level, Teddy has to lean forward to see past Adam in the driver's seat. What the fuck, Teddy says, awake now. Are they playing Snap? The girl is wearing gold earrings that catch the light. With a shriek she brings her hand down and beats the flimsy table, making it shake. The guy laughs even harder and says something to her like *careful now*. He catches a bottle as it rolls from the table, spilling something on his hands, which he then flicks at her. Maybe they're drunk. When Adam switches the engine off their voices are clearer. The guy has an accent

Teddy can't place. They must know they're being watched, but they still haven't acknowledged the truck or the two boys, men, inside. You'll get the cards dirty, the girl squeals. Adam shouts across the road, Are you folks broken down? They don't seem to hear, though perhaps now there's some deliberateness to their actions, like they can sense being on display. Something about the scene unsettles Teddy, who starts to tell Adam they should keep driving. But Adam has already unclipped his belt and is opening the door, his question still hanging in the air. He climbs out and turns, his eyes finding Teddy's through the open window. Let's fuck with them, Adam says.

FUCK WITH THEM how? asks Teddy, but Adam can't think further than fuck, that girl is beautiful man, like truly. Her hair is dead straight, the colour girls at school call dirty blonde. How is it so neat if she slept in that van last night? It stops in a clean line on her sleeveless arm. Tank top. Bra? He has her in profile, laughing on one side of a folding picnic table, washed in sunlight beside a yellow hippie van with a pop-top. Engine in the back. Adam hates vehicles like that—they're for people who for some reason want to live shiny plastic versions of their grandparents' lives. But there's something about the way her head curves and then drops into that cute jut of a nose. When girls laugh they look either pretty or mean, and this one is in the first category, no question. After a glance she ignores Adam again; she's laughing with or at the long-haired guy. Boyfriend. Makeup? No lipstick, but her eyelashes are sharp as creatures, oddly black below the lighter brown of her brows. Mascara. It's crazy how much he's unwillingly learned from the people he despises at school. The book says this phenomenon is a close relation of indoctrination. It says we should be conscious of external influences, and something about training your mind to be adsorbent rather than absorbent, which Adam assumes just means be on your guard. But the girl is wearing mascara by the side of the highway, and in this moment Adam is happy to know it. He runs his fingers through his hair. If they are broken down, they don't look too concerned. They're playing cards. It's like watching a couple of bear cubs, they're so wrapped up in their game they don't notice the man across the road in camo pants and boots, observing. Adam feels cool air against his sweaty back and a moment later the same breeze lifts the girl's hair from her shoulder. Fuck with them *how*, Teddy says again, and Adam ignores him again. He wants to see if he can get their attention just by staring. The guy flexes the cards in front of his chest like knuckles before a fight. The girl puts a silver bottle to her lips but doesn't drink. Do it more, Adam hears her say. That's not enough, don't cheat, oh my god you've got to learn to *shuffle*. Her voice is Californian fried. When the guy tries to start dealing, she grabs his wrists and Adam notices they wear matching plastic bracelets, the kind you get at a music festival or a hospital. It is the fluorescent orange bracelets and the holding of wrists that make Adam slightly, and inexplicably, angry. They nudge him further into his game. He thinks he hears another car approaching, but it is only the wind. The girl takes the cards from the guy and begins to shuffle expertly, her wrists twisting as she cuts and neatens the two halves of deck. Now who taught her that? Not the one she's with now, clearly. One of the ones that came before. Adam watches her work. It would not be too much to say he is mesmerized. Whatever happens next, Adam will have watched the deck moving smoothly and mechanically between her fingers, seen the silver ring on her thumb, heard the satisfying *thruck* of cards interlacing on the table. He has been granted access to a secret, along with the people who know her and know about this skill of hers. It is intimacy of a kind.

Partly Adam enjoys watching without being noticed, but another part of him aches for the guy, especially the guy, to ask him what his problem is. There is no earthly way this guy does not know Adam is standing there. Maybe he is too afraid to interact. Two lanes of blacktop make twenty-four feet, with a broken line down the middle. Adam has worked out what annoys him about these two. All that laughing and touching reminds him of an insurance ad that runs constantly when his dad watches late-night TV. Adam has been in the room enough times to know it by heart, another thing that has colonized his mind. The next scene would be them hugging, the woman's arms wrapped around the guy's neck, a pregnancy test tight in her fist. If that was real the test would have piss all over it, Adam's dad said once, ending a stretch of silence between them that might have been going all day. Michael could be funny when he wanted to be. Adam felt like reaching into the TV and dragging the two actors out onto the living room floor, to show them that life does not trot from one happy scene to another, from pregnancy test to Little League to graduation, on a bridge of orthodontic smiles.

Okay she is finally, *finally*, looking at him, her lips around the bottle, her head back. Adam thinks he can see her throat ripple as she drinks. He tries to hold her gaze, to make her look away first. The guy is pretending to be oblivious, slapping cards onto the table, his face still reflecting the smile that was on hers before she drank. She says a quiet something to the guy, and he looks up. There are little piles of cards in front of each of them. Adam steps into the road. You folks need a hand? he calls. Long-hair answers, and Adam needs a moment to understand what was said. No-thanks-pal-we're-fine, it all sounds like one word, like the Arabs in Patriot. The girl sounds American but this guy with his *nothankspal*... Britain, he thinks, Scotland, or Ireland. Adam, in the middle of the road, turns his back on them. Teddy's still just sitting in the truck, his arms in a shrug like *what are we even doing here, what is your plan?* Loud enough so all three can hear, Adam asks Teddy: Is that guy even speaking English? Teddy smiles, unclips his belt, and leans across Adam's seat to the open window. Adam steps back to give Teddy a clear shot. Teddy leans out the window and shouts, Do you speak English? Adam and Teddy laugh.

The guy doesn't seem to know what's going on, but puts his cards face-down on the table and tries to get up. Unfortunately for him, he has to shuffle his pink folding chair back before he has room to stand. We're okay, no bother, he calls. Flooded the engine but she'll be fine in a bit. It's probably good to go but we're just taking a break. The girl whips the line of hair off her shoulder and says plastically, Thanks so much for stopping, though. She looks away, picks up her cards, and studies them too carefully.

Adam turns to Teddy and says, Did you see him wink when he said *taking a break*? Teddy nods but looks confused. He is still sprawled across the driver's seat. Get out of the truck, Adam says quietly. Teddy stares for a moment, then shrugs and says, I need to piss anyway. He scoots back to his own side and opens the passenger door.

The couple are once more at their game. As Adam closes the distance between him and them, he calls, Looks like you guys are a long way from home, mimicking the girl's accent without meaning to. We can help you get back on the road. Looks like you're driving a real piece of shit, though. It's probably fine around here with people passing by who can help, but you should be careful if you plan on going remote in that thing. Plus I wouldn't just leave your food sprawled everywhere like that. Don't they have bears where you're from? Adam has said all this while crossing the remainder of the road. Closer up the girl is less pretty. There are blue moons of dirt beneath her fingernails, just like the ones under Adam's own. A dirty blonde. The guy just smiles dumbly, and Adam can tell he doesn't want to start any kind of back and forth, but the girl goes ahead and says, We know what we're doing, thank you. That gives Adam the chance to say, Are you carrying a firearm, in case you need to scare off a bear? No we don't have a *gun*, she says, in a way that lets him know what kind of girl she is. A girl like Brianna and Grace and all that sort. Condescending. Who don't understand they're sharing the world with others. Adam listens for a car, but everything's quiet, except for the sound of Teddy's urine puddling the earth.

The man lets Adam know that they're *not idiots*, that they have bear spray, and tells him to *have a nice day*. But Adam keeps staring at them. He's on their side of the road now, just barely in what might be considered their personal space. For effect, he doesn't turn his head when he calls out, Hey Teddy. There is a silence, which Adam assumes is also for effect, then Teddy calls from behind: What? These two don't have a gun, Adam says.

That does it. The long-haired guy shifts around the table toward the girl, catches his foot on his folding chair and topples it. He is trying to act strong. They are probably all about the same age, the four of them. Maybe these two are a little older. Just for the fun of it, Adam puts on his soft, reasonable voice and says, You should have brought one.

Adam doesn't feel heat building inside him. He feels cool and clean after the warm stink of the truck. The sweat on his T-shirt is almost dry. He knows he will be able to hear another vehicle long before it gets close. Apart from a hush of leaves and the low hum of summer flies, it is mostly quiet. Every now and then a bird cries a warning. Long-hair finally makes it around the table to his girlfriend. He is clearly getting scared, which is the most perfect and wonderful thing. It means Adam is pitching a perfect game. The guy deserves to be scared, he should be. He cannot go through life assuming everyone is his friend. Adam and Teddy are probably doing him a favour, jerking him out of whatever machine he lives in. Even if this guy doesn't know it, he is only out here so he can go back to wherever he's from and tell his friends how amazing it was here, how he hooked up with this hot American girl; he will watch their eyes while he tells the precious story, pausing every now and then to make them wait for a good bit, while they sit around drinking warm beer in their depressing town. Now he can add the bit about the two crazy locals they ran into on the road, and how he genuinely feared for his life. Why not give him a splash of chilled water, a nudge to make the story even better? The guy crouches next to the girl and says something Adam cannot hear. Don't touch her, Adam decides to say. The guy looks sharply at Adam, anger and fear grappling in his eyes, and finally anger wins and he says as he stands erect, Fuck off, pal—this happens to be my fucking girlfriend and we're minding our own business so how about you do the same and piss off up the road. Don't touch her, Adam says again, softly, just to see what will happen. What makes it the perfect thing to say is that the guy *isn't* touching her, so he's obeying to begin with. And if he were to touch her, it would be somehow shitty, unboyfriendly. It would have everything to do with Adam and nothing to do with the girl herself. Adam can hardly believe he stumbled onto something so good. Behind him he hears the door of the truck open. Probably on the far side, out of sight. Yes, Teddy. The girl has her hands on her armrests like she can't decide whether to stand up or not. Please go away, she says. There's no problem, we just want to be left alone, okay? She is as reasonable as a kindergarten teacher. It almost works—Adam almost feels ashamed. Girls are smart like that: they'll always give you a way out, a chance to stop before it's too late. Even when it *is* too late, they try to convince you it isn't. Most guys take the way out when it's offered. Adam understands she is offering it to her boyfriend as much as to him, that she is, in some tiny and unarticulated way, afraid of her boyfriend as well as of Adam. But the guy steps toward him and says, loudly, What possible right do you have to tell me not to touch my own girlfriend? What earthly business is that of yours? Then he stops. Something is coming. A car makes itself heard, and Adam has to step toward his opponent as an suv approaches and slows. Now would be the time, if things had gone that far, for the couple to rush into the road and ask for help. But things, Adam calculates, have stopped just short of that, and he is right. The three of them watch the white car pass. Adam sees the driver looking out at them, curious and unconcerned. It's a woman, oldish, with messy curly hair that might be grey. She accelerates, and the white car is soon out of earshot and sight. When it's quiet again Adam hears the truck door slam, and the girl gets slowly to her feet. She's more graceful than her boyfriend. Adam is enjoying the fact that he cannot see where Teddy is, having to trust that his friend has his back. He tries to concentrate on the two people in front of him, to notice each movement, however small, relaxing his mind until he is sure nothing they might do will surprise him. The guy backs away until he reaches the girl and puts his arm around her. Just as Adam hoped, the gesture is staged, done more for Adam's benefit than hers. They look idiotic. What do you want? the girl suddenly shouts, more frightened than Adam could have made her. The man says nothing but his mouth drops open. Adam realizes that neither of them is quite looking at him anymore. Their shoulders are angled like they don't know which way to twist, as though the wind were blowing them backwards. Only now does Adam allow himself to accept his victory, to break the stare and turn to look at Teddy, though he already knows what he will see.

A DROP OF piss must have hit Teddy's right boot; he can sense the dark stain even though his eyes are locked on the British guy's startled face. There is the sound of flies, and a large bird flying over his head. There's Adam, staring at him in shock or admiration or relief or all three; there's the girl, looking like she's been frozen in the middle of a dance move. Teddy knows all this without taking his focus off the guy, whose eyes, he decides, are too far apart on his face, his head a bit too square, weird looking, especially with the long hair. They are all looking at Teddy, except the bird, who clearly has somewhere to be and flies on over the trees.

Until a couple of days ago Teddy had only ever held a gun at the range where he did his safety and handling course. That was two years ago; his father had driven him through the rain and waited the whole time for him in the parking lot. ACTS and PROVE, acronyms he learned that day and whose meanings he has since forgotten. The laminated permit he got is in Adam's truck now, in the pocket of what Teddy's mother calls his summer coat. See the boy, pointing his brand new SKS rifle at a stranger without even knowing why. He loaded the magazine while listening to Adam talk, the coolness of metal calming him, helping him avoid thinking about what would happen next. The breeze presses at Teddy's face, making him aware of the wispy hair that covers his cheeks. He can smell unspent fuel and soil and wet pine needles. Everybody is being quiet and waiting for him to say or do the next thing. Whatever it is that comes after you point a gun at someone. Teddy's eyes flick to Adam and back to his target. Adam is just baskingly looking on, which is no help. Of course, what happens next must be up to Teddy. The man with the gun gets to decide. Has to decide. But the longer this goes on, the more he invites someone else to fill his silence for him. Teddy, having felt so controlled a moment ago, begins to panic.

Long-haired guy has a bracelet and an eyebrow piercing and he takes two steps forward, letting go of the girl and stumbling into a sentence. His voice has gone high like a child's, or like he's struggling to breathe. Let's—let's calm down, okay? Let's both just drive away. We won't tell anyone. Let's both just—please. The word *both* bothers Teddy; it sounds inaccurate, makes it seem like he and Adam are one person.

Teddy, still unable to speak, decides on an experiment. He moves the rifle a fraction left until it is pointing at the girl, then, after a terrifying rush of vertigo, edges it back again. She makes a noise no human should make, more like a sheep or a cow. Teddy has momentarily made her animal. What do you want? the guy says, still high and breathless. It's a decent question and it has too many answers. Teddy wants nothing, the true, irreversible kind of nothing. He wants not to have dribbled piss on his nice new boots. He wants to check into a motel with Adam, to take show-ers and then watch a shitty daytime movie and get drunk on twin beds. To spend all their money in a couple of days and arrive home victorious, with stories to tell. To please Adam, who would probably like it if they stole these folks' car. They could drive both vehicles up the road a bit and then set fire to the van, or else swap over and burn Adam's truck to the ground. But what if the van won't start? Worse, what if Teddy doesn't have it in him to drive it? At any moment somebody else might come past and see him holding a gun. He almost wants that to happen, especially if it's a carful of guys on a hunting or fishing trip. At least then he wouldn't have to decide. Someone would shout at him to drop it, and he would. Why doesn't Adam or long-hair shout that? That's all it would take, but they're both just watching uselessly. Finally, Adam and the other guy do join forces and come to the rescue. The guy's been edging closer to the girl again, reaching a blind arm out, and Adam says in a low, almost friendly voice, I told you not to touch her.

Teddy feels breath leave his body. The focus is elsewhere, at least for the moment. Now he is back riding shotgun again, like when they're driving. Long-hair says, Listen, go have your fun somewhere else and leave us alone. He's still reaching toward his girlfriend, stalled somewhere between submission and defi-ance. He's been split three ways now: eyes on Teddy's rifle, arm toward the girl, Adam's words in his ears. The girl's arms are cov-ering her breasts. She looks too frightened to grasp that there are rules to this game. Her lips are moving desperately, but she's not saying words. She doesn't seem to have any idea that her boyfriend is even there. She only has eyes for Teddy, and maybe a glance or two for Adam. At any moment she might take a breath and scream louder than any of them would give her credit for. Adam turns his back fully on Teddy, and stepping almost into Teddy's shot, says to the couple, Move away from the road. Back up toward the trees. Turn around and walk. Now. Do it. The guy tries to stare Adam down, not moving, but the girl takes a step back and falls without a sound onto her butt. When the guy swivels to help her up, Teddy hears himself scream, Get-away-from-her-don't-touch-her. The words echo in his head, and he realizes with shame that his voice isn't low like a man's. It too has turned childish. But it does the trick because the guy freezes, looking at Teddy with proper hatred now, which relieves Teddy, gives him a reason to hate back. The three men watch the woman as she gets first to her knees, then manages to pull herself into a crouch. She holds herself like that, like a boulder; her hair has fallen over her face and she does not shift it. Teddy likes that, knowing that she can't see him anymore. The guy, her boyfriend, says something to her, but she doesn't respond, just holds her knees, shoulders shaking in a silent sob. Adam, Teddy says, lowering the rifle, let's go. But Adam doesn't hear him, or pretends not to. Ceecee is going to be afraid of Teddy when this story gets told. Of course she'll break up with him, but she was always going to. There's no way they last to the end of high school. He's sensed for a while that her sights are set higher than him. This will just give her an easy way out. Teddy will become a story Ceecee tells other guys, until she either gets sick of their reactions or runs out of guys to tell it to. The psycho ex. He isn't sad or angry about it: the gun's weight has numbed him. The girl squatting in front of him looks small, pathetic, with her necklace hanging outside her top, her dusty shorts and her flip-flops, head in her hands, fingers in her hair, that ring on her thumb. When they were little, he and Grace used to play like that, squatting rather than sitting, and Teddy's mother said it must be because of their Indian blood.

Adam has been saying things to the guy, who is now pulling the girl to her feet. They're walking backwards, awkwardly, toward the trees. Teddy is spectating now, not really aiming anywhere. He watches the girl lose a flip-flop and almost steps forward to pick it up for her. They turn their backs and walk away more quickly, and Adam shoots Teddy a look that says *come on buddy, keep up*. Teddy feels like he's been caught not paying attention in class. He points the rifle back where it's supposed to be. The four of them move away from the road toward a grassy drainage ditch that runs between the trees and the asphalt. As he passes, Adam upends the pink table, scattering bottles and playing cards. The pattern on the back of each card is blue and white lace, machine-printed, centred and symmetrical. Last year their math teacher brought a bunch of decks into class when they were doing probability. Suits and numbers, red and black, impossible calculations, irredeemably limp. Teddy puts the rifle up to his shoulder and stares over the sight. He walks more confidently now, like his own avatar. He can hear the girl saying, Please god somebody come just somebody drive past please help us god please. They are gripping hands now, in spite of Adam's order. Or Adam must have decided to allow it. Their rigid and shaking wrists make Teddy want to scream don't-touch-her again, but what comes out is some kind of trilled yelp that makes Adam look at him in surprise. Adam is smiling, though, probably assuming this is part of Teddy's act: the crazy, unpredictable man. Adam waits for Teddy to come level. See the boys, side by side, finally. The guy and the girl have reached the ditch and are looking into it. Adam slips into Teddy's shadow, close enough for his words to dowse Teddy's burning ear. This is enough, Adam says quietly to his friend. The guy turns to face them. Please, he screams. Adam says to Teddy, Now we can . . . But he says nothing after that. There is a pause like Adam is thinking, like he has them all arranged like chess pieces, Teddy included, and is considering his next move. More quietly, the boyfriend says, Stay calm. He could be saying it to Teddy or Adam, or to the girl, or even to himself. Stay calm, he says again. Stay calm. He keeps repeating it with every breath, stopping only when Teddy shoots him in the chest and he falls backwards. The girl makes another animal noise and stumbles down into the ditch after the guy, taking a great strangled gulp of air. Her arms reach for the guy but her legs do not stop not even for a moment; they are already taking her along the length of the ditch, as birds tumble into the sky, flies still buzzing as though it means zero to them, the girl running the ditch and whining. This only lasts a second or so, then Teddy shoots twice more and she falls too.

Just three rounds. Probably neither of them is dead. Call an ambulance, Teddy thinks. There won't be reception, he thinks. Now I shoot myself, he thinks. Adam will know what to do, he thinks. He taps his pocket in that unconscious way, to check that his phone is there. The gun seems no longer to be in his hands.

His ears are ringing and he can see a shell on the ground and the girl's torso moving up and down, up and down. That's a relief. As he backs away from the ditch, the guy and girl fall nicely out of sight. He brings his hands to his face and Adam's arms must be around him because he hasn't fallen down. Adam says, We have to get the fuck, man. Somebody's going to come past. Hold it together just for a minute. Adam has his hot palm in Teddy's armpit. But Teddy is too heavy and soon they have slumped nearly to their knees. That was fucking amazing, Adam says. Now let's get back to the truck. Okay, Teddy says. Adam heaves them to their feet and tells Teddy what to do. He seems unbelievably calm. He picks up the gun with one hand and with his other arm around Teddy they walk across the road and to the passenger side, as though Adam were a medic and Teddy the one who'd been shot. Adam helps Teddy up and in and then tries to get the rifle between Teddy's legs and under the passenger seat, but it won't go, the angle's not right, the barrel won't clear the glove box. Soon Adam is pushing it so carelessly that Teddy comes to himself and says, Whoa, whoa, careful. Teddy thrusts it back at Adam like a toddler declining food. He hears movement behind him. The door slams shut and Teddy watches Adam run in front of the windshield. He watches his friend right the picnic table and lower the van's hood. Adam leans through the driver's window and the hazards stop blinking. Then he jogs to the ditch and disappears into it. Teddy closes his eyes, knowing that when he opens them there will be the speck of a vehicle rounding the bend ahead. Engine after engine approaches through the hum of wind and trees. Somewhere, a bird protests all this. Then a fresh certainty, that Adam is not coming back, that he's run into the forest to play would-be-victim-number-three, descends. Teddy counts back from twenty, knowing that at zero Adam will still be gone and he will have to open his eyes onto a new situation. By eleven he hears the sound of boots on the road, Adam's door opening and closing, the relief of the truck starting up, the feeling of being pushed back in his seat as Adam drives.

Teddy opens his eyes a moment later, before Adam has even made it into third, when the truck lurches to a stop in the road. He looks and listens wildly, trying to locate the latest panic. Adam says nothing but calmly unclips his own buckle and reaches past Teddy's throat to the seat belt, which he pulls, smoothly and without it snagging even once, across Teddy's body.

THE WAY THEY curved like Alpha-Bits in the bowl, the fact that that was what Adam thought of, the milky dregs of childhood Saturdays, his favourite cereal with its mutant letters as well as real ones, random twists that might have been secret code, the girl face down, one arm cocked like she was waving to someone underground, hair all twisted and fanned, a bra strap cutting briefly out from the ruined tank top before ducking back inside. The guy, face up but with all that hair over him like a blindfold, making desperate wordless noise when Adam came back from depositing Teddy in the passenger seat. Adam was magically and invincibly calm as he took a knee in the damp ditch, took a breath, and reached toward the man's pocket. There was less blood than he expected. He pulled his tongue down from the roof of his mouth, which the book says is something to be aware of. For a moment the guy's moaning turned accusatory, then it settled into a slow whine, like gas escaping through a too-small hole. Adam didn't have to think about what he was doing: it was simply what would happen next. He made sure not to hold his breath as he tightened his grip and gently pulled, the back of his thumb sensing warmth through the pocket lining. Thankfully the guy kept his wallet in the front of his jeans, not against his ass where Adam kept his. It was nearly free when something shifted, the blindfold slipped, and Adam could see a single, accosting eye. He let go of the wallet and retreated in a crouch to escape the guy's line of sight. But the horrible pale eye didn't notice him or didn't care; it was looking either at the blank sky or the swaying tops of the pines. Adam thinks now, as he leans on the accelerator, that the guy probably had better things to worry about in that moment than him or Teddy. Maybe it was the exact moment he bled out, because by the time Adam forced himself back to the body, there was no more movement and no more sound. He reached toward the guy's crotch without looking and got the wallet free in a moment. Then he was gone. He couldn't try the girl. He might tell himself now that it was chivalry, but really he didn't want to look too closely. She was bloodier than the guy was. He was pretty sure Teddy had gotten her twice. He remembers three shots. Only three, and Teddy had barely fired a gun before. There will be time to lay out horror, pride, and envy side by side, with neat borders between them, as though they might grow and one day be harvested. There will be time to decide, to revise. Girls' clothes don't have pockets anyway, he thinks, at least not ones big enough to keep anything valuable in.

The sun is going. Adam is beginning to speed. He touches the brake and shifts back in his seat. He tries to keep his mind on the what-happens-now, but he can't help picturing the logo on her tank top, a woman's face made up of a hundred tiny lines, with maybe the name of a university below. For some reason he wishes he could remember what school it was. They've been driving for an hour and still haven't passed anyone. If they're lucky, nobody will pass the van until it's dark, and it will be tomorrow before anybody notices. They need to be far away by then. That is his job now, to deliver Teddy. Thinking that calms him. Adam takes his sunglasses off and dumps them in the door pocket, beside the wallet. The trees here are thick on both sides; Adam can't see what's around the next bend until he gets there. He glances at Teddy, who has his hands pressed between his legs and still hasn't said a word. But he seems calm, bored even. He's just staring on the diagonal, occasionally tracking a tree or rock as it sails by. Maybe he's pretending nothing happened, that they never stopped driving. Adam has tried to bring him out of it. He has said, That was fucking wild, and punched the roof between them. He has said, It'll be okay, man, it'll be a thousand kinds of fine. Now he tries again: Honestly fuck them, they provoked you. Still Teddy doesn't respond, and Adam immediately regrets saying *you* instead of *us*. If they're going to get clear, and Adam has decided they are, then they need to be a unit. Adam needs to take his share of responsibility. Maybe that's why he was inspired to go back for the wallet, to prove to Teddy and himself that he is implicated too. His left hand slips into the door pocket and touches leather. The guy's name is Alexander Shankland; it felt important to find that out. There was no blood on the wallet. Adam was relieved by that at first, but now wonders if he isn't slightly disappointed, because there is nowhere else to go but forward. There's a good bit of cash inside, a surprising amount, even for a tourist. A credit card, too, though Adam wouldn't know the first thing about using it. Probably a rookie mistake to try. He hasn't told Teddy about the wallet yet, or the Jack he pulled out of the grass by the van. Taking it was probably childish, but he had a wild thought it would be like a serial killer's calling card, but in reverse. The cops would be bagging up evidence and somebody would work out that one card was missing from the deck. They'd search the ground, but they wouldn't find it. Adam could almost laugh out loud imagining that, a bunch of men in uniforms asking one another what the hell it could mean. He swallows a mouthful of soda and puts the bottle between his thighs.

But he shouldn't have thought about police: now every curve feels as though it will open onto flashing lights. If they're not being hunted already, they soon will be. He needs to use this time to work things out. The tank is only a third full, plus they never got around to filling the red canister he bought the day they left. So the first step is to stop somewhere, before anyone finds out what happened, and fill up to the absolute brim. They can ditch the water in the blue canister and fill that with gas too. Then they'll take the smallest roads, keep heading north, and stay there. Thinking the plan through a second time relaxes him again. It fractures into keywords he can repeat like a mantra. Gas station, blue canister, more food, small roads, north.

And who actually saw them, anyway? Just that one old woman in the white SUV, the woman with the hair. And that was before anything even happened. She would have seen a truck and a van on either side of the road, Adam stepping onto the shoulder, facing the couple at their camp table. Adam is the one she might remember; Teddy was probably hidden by the truck. She might have sensed that words were being exchanged, but she has probably forgotten all about it. Adam's truck might stick in her mind. He has always liked the fact that it's conspicuous, red and black with the camper shell looming over it like a cloud.

That woman who passed us, Adam says aloud, the white car that went past . . . Listen, we can be witnesses just like her. Teddy turns to him but says nothing. Yeah, listen, Adam goes on. This is what we do. If anyone asks, we drove by just like the woman did. We saw exactly what she saw. A truck and a hippie van on either side of the road, and some people standing around. We make it close to how the driver of the white car is going to describe it, but just different enough to confuse everyone. Two dudes, a truck that looked like mine except maybe we say the colour was different. Maybe it was brown instead of red. And we're sure about that because we would have noticed if they were exactly the same. Adam doesn't know if Teddy's even listening, but he goes on talking. Maybe we make them Native guys. Or foreigners. Just one or two details, like maybe one had black hair. One had a jean jacket, stuff that makes them different to us but not so it'd be weird that we remember the details. Teddy turns back to his own window and says, We have to get rid of the gun. We throw it in the river or we bury it. When it's dark. Adam says confidently, Don't worry about that. I know what to do. He digs his thumb into his thigh, where the bruise Teddy gave him days ago is beginning to be less responsive. Which is a shame, because he has gotten used to pressing on it. There's no way we're getting rid of the gun, he thinks. Not yet.

Adam tells Teddy they will get the fuck and stay out of sight for a while. He tells Teddy to make sure their phones are switched off. They pull off the road, and he spreads the map across the dash, tracing the line of their escape with a dirty finger. When he stows the rifle under the wadded tarpaulin in the back, Teddy slumps into nodding compliance and doesn't mention it again. Later, they pass a road sign showing another two hundred to Mugg Creek and the stylized little pump that means gas. If they can fill up and get clear, they'll be properly in the wilderness by tomorrow. Then it will be a different sort of game. But first thing's first. Halfway around the next curve there are headlights, somebody coming toward them, driving south. Adam stops thinking, drops the high beams, sits up straight, puts both hands on the wheel, stares hard at his side of the road. The other vehicle passes harmlessly, like a wave. It's gone too quickly to tell what it was. Glancing at the taillights in the rear-view Adam realizes his tongue is on the roof of his mouth again. He puts his headlights back up and accelerates. Something, a countdown or a race, has started.

THE SIGN OUTSIDE the Mugg Creek Gas Lodge has the word
SAVE in fat fluorescent letters above the prices of gas and diesel
and the words LOWER THAN ANDERTON LAKE, GOOD FOOD,
TOWING, 24/365 WE NEVER CLOSE, AFTER HOURS SOUND
HORN. The truck's headlights pick out cornflowers in the long
grass as it turns toward a pair of unbranded pumps. At 3:09 on
the emerald dashboard clock, Adam kills the engine and suddenly Teddy can hear his own breath. Looks pretty closed, Adam
says as he performs a two-fisted stretch. Teddy cups his eyes
against the cold truck window. It looks more like somebody's
house than a gas station, dark except for one exterior light giving a weak, energy-saving glow to a planter of flowers and a rack
of propane. Teddy says, The sign back there said to sound your
horn, I guess to wake them up. Jeez, Adam says. We really are
in the Dark Ages. For another moment they are side by side in
the dark. The interior light will not come on until one of them
opens his door.

Outside, Teddy breathes a comforting smell of engine and
tires. The moon is long gone. There are still a stupid amount of
stars, but the sky is turning purple on one side, another sunrise

getting ready to go. Adam said they would have to be off the highway by dawn, onto a smaller road he has found on the map, which avoids Anderton Lake and takes them north, farther into nowhere. Adam said this would be the last place they'd stop. Teddy didn't say, The last place 'til *when*? He didn't say that eventually they would run out of gas. They would run out of water and Adam's dad's canned food. They would run out of north to drive into. Adam was cold and concentrated, not to be disagreed with, as though this were a test and he had studied. The only challenge Teddy could muster was to ask what if there were security cameras at the gas station, wouldn't somebody be able to read the truck's plates and get pictures of their faces and such? Adam seemed glad Teddy had asked such a stupid question. Cameras? People out here don't have technology, man. Anyway, what choice do we have? It's not like the truck runs on your farts. Teddy didn't laugh, just wondered that there could still be jokes after what had happened and was grateful that there could.

It's impossible to walk up to a quiet building at night without feeling like a criminal. Teddy even feels it at his own house sometimes, when the noise of Adam's truck fades and he picks his wasted way between the snails on the side path, past Grace's bedroom window toward the kitchen door. Adam was right about there not being security cameras, at least. There's nothing high-tech here. A sawn-off barrel filled with pink flowers, a chalkboard sign with the heading FOOD TO GO and nothing written below. Adam appears beside him and whispers, You good? Teddy nods, letting his fingers trail through the flowers. Either there was dew or they were watered recently. He tells himself he will not be a liability. On the way here Adam had wondered aloud whether Teddy should lie in the back with the tarp spread over him, to make it seem like Adam was travelling alone, but then decided it was too risky, that it would be far worse if anyone noticed. They didn't know the gas station would be as dark and lonely as this. Teddy would have much preferred to lie in the camper and play dead, to cover himself up, but he is not in charge. He has put his fingers in his mouth and is absently sucking the moisture from them. They taste of metal, not flowers. When was the last time he drank anything? Finally a light goes on somewhere, and the building seems to exhale. Adam grinds a toe through the gravel and says, Places like this aren't going to survive much longer. Teddy transfers his hands to his pockets. At least they have plenty of money now. Adam showed him how much was in the guy's wallet when they pulled over to study the map. Drinks on me, Adam said, fanning the red and brown bills like a hand of cards. Teddy felt briefly like spewing and closed his eyes to fight it off. He didn't know why Adam would make a joke out of it. Either to make Teddy feel better, or to make him feel worse.

The woman is talking to them before she has even opened the door. Morning, boys, she says, then something else that Teddy does not catch. When she reaches up to release a bolt above the door, the metal zipper of her fleece jacket scrapes the glass as her chest crushes against it. The lock clicks, and she steps outside like she has been expecting them all night. Sorry to keep you waiting, she says, zipping the fleece jacket right to the neck. Sure is cold for July, huh? But then I say that every year, so I guess it's not. The words whirl around Teddy, who wants to be unmemorable but also to not say anything at all, incompatible impulses. He looks to Adam, who saves him with a polite, Hey there, sorry to wake you. The woman has grey-brown hair and a fold on each side of her mouth. Her eyes have that swollen, just-woke-up look, but she slaps her butt cheerfully and asks what Teddy and Adam need. Adam says to fill up with gas. His tone says he's not in a talking mood. It'll take a minute to wake the pump up, she says. Come out of the chill if you like. The best Teddy manages is to resist putting his fingers back in his mouth. We're fine out here, Adam says, and for a brief moment the woman looks at Teddy, as if to ask whether he is happy being spoken for. Teddy turns help-lessly toward the truck, and the tarpaulin he'd rather be under. He crosses his arms to rub his biceps through his long-sleeved T-shirt. It must be the thing they learned about in geography, how it actually gets colder right as the sun comes up. When he squeezes his own arms, it is as though somebody else is touch-ing him, holding him safely across the chest. He releases himself only when he hears a sound from above. It's juicy, bad, not a regular cough. It goes on for a few strokes, like an engine try-ing to start, then the gas pump begins to hum and click and the old woman is back. For a moment she stands with her hands on either side of the doorway, staring up at the ceiling. Whoever it is chokes a final breath and is quiet. The woman goes on looking up at what must be ceiling panels, and Teddy goes on watching her. Her throat is a pattern of folds and flaps, a little landscape she wouldn't see unless she looked in a mirror. Adam is over by the truck, not paying attention. Eventually she sighs and says to Teddy, He has to sleep sitting up. Teddy tries to think of something inconsequential to say. I hope he's okay, he manages. The lesson is don't smoke, the woman says. At least not as much as he did. I guess you all vape these days, but eventually they'll discover that's just as bad. Teddy, as though hypnotized, says, I don't vape. The woman says, Good boy. Teddy turns away and puts his arms back across his chest.

Adam is trying to release the gas nozzle, but the woman stops him in a boss-mom kind of way. It's not self-service here. Yes ma'am, Adam says, holding up both hands and backing off. I guess you want it full, she says. Yes please, Adam says. We have a couple of canisters too. Teddy has his fingers back in his mouth, two from each hand. At any moment she is going to ask them where they're headed, because that is what friendly people at backwater gas stations do in the middle of the night. Teddy worries Adam will use his name, like to tell him to fetch the gas canister. He decides to get it before Adam can ask. Inside the truck he leans across the tarpaulin and undoes the elastic cord that holds the canister in place. He pictures the woman's soft throat again. He imagines her husband coughing blood on her. He imagines having to listen to a person slowly suffocate, over months or maybe years. Teddy doesn't know why, but he runs his hand over the tarp in a way that Adam can surely hear. He can feel the rifle through the plastic. The old woman is about three feet away. The thought that this might freak Adam out and make him, Teddy, seem dangerous and unpredictable, calms him. It reminds him that they are playing a game. But when he gets back with the canister, Adam doesn't even make eye contact, just says: Go get the other one too, pour out the water. Again the woman looks at Teddy, curious that he's being bossed around like this. She says, I suppose it'd be rude of me to tell you you'll get sick if you drink the river water around here. It's okay, Adam lies, we have an extra one. The woman says nothing more. She is distracted by the coughing, which has started up again and can be heard even over the noise of the pump. Teddy lugs their water canister to a patch of grass and pours it out over the cornflowers. Behind him the woman's voice says, So, you boys are heading north? Teddy just freezes there, letting the gas pump and the incessant coughing and the glugging water fill the silence. Luckily, he's far enough away not to be expected to answer. Yeah, Adam says eventually. Heading up to work for the summer. The woman says, You're leaving that a bit late, aren't you? Not a whole lot of summer left. Teddy stares down the other side of the circular drive toward the highway and realizes how stupid Adam is. What they should have done is gone right past this place, waited half an hour, then turned around and driven in from the north. They could have told the lady they'd *come* from Anderton Lake. Then drive south, wait half an hour, U-turn, and drive past again when she's back in bed listening to her husband cough up his lung. This is why he shouldn't trust Adam with their decisions. A voice, maybe his father's, tells him to wake up.

When he returns with the empty canister, Adam is stretching as though he's tired from the drive and nothing more. The woman hasn't said anything else; she's watching the price on the pump click upwards.

We saw something weird earlier on, Adam says when he's done stretching. Teddy looks at him, and Adam looks solidly back. Some kind of argument going on, Adam says. Yeah, Teddy adds, but after that he's lost. On the other side of a giant, deafening pause, the woman says, It's a beautiful place to come have an argument. The road, I mean. My husband always says that's why couples go on trips, so they can have a year's worth of fights in one hit. He says there's a certain kind of argument you can only have when you're at a crossroads, looking at a map. She laughs softly to herself, releasing the trigger on the gas pump, and her eyes shift toward the window again. He says GPS is going to make the divorce rate go up, she goes on, because people need to get lost every now and then. It wasn't like that, Adam says hesitatingly, and Teddy can feel him deciding whether to give up or press on. Teddy begins to panic. He wonders what it will take to get Adam to shut up. The first full gas canister is right there by his feet. He should screw the cap back on but is afraid she will see his fingers shaking. He kicks a stone that ends up scooting right to the woman's shoe. We think it was some kind of road rage, Adam says. A light has gone on in the upstairs window, and the woman is not listening. She has to bend over slightly to slot the nozzle into the water canister. To nobody in particular, she says, My son's coming up here with his family next week, on vacation. Little does he know I'm going to put him right to work. Maybe my grandson too. She laughs her sad laugh again, and the three of them stand there alone, waiting for the last canister to fill. When the throaty sound indicates it is nearly full, she says, You boys need anything else, coffee or snacks? Normally we do food, but my husband is the chef and as you can hear he's out of order right now. She says that even though the coughing has stopped. Adam pulls his wallet, his own wallet, from his back pocket and says, We're good, thanks. The woman holds the dripping nozzle away from her body and for a moment she just stands there watching the drops hit the ground. She might be the mother of the world. And having been so desperate to get away from this place, from this woman, Teddy finds himself saying, I'll take a coffee. That snaps the woman back from wherever she had gone. She holsters the nozzle and pulls two paper towels from the dispenser, wiping her hands. Okey dokey, she says. Come on inside.

POOR TEDDY, ADAM finds himself thinking as he drives. Poor Teddy, because he keeps falling asleep, for a few seconds or a minute, but always wakes up again before long. They haven't had more than a piss break since the gas station, which feels like days ago. The sun is already heavy and looming above the truck, and the inside of Adam's door is too hot for his elbow. When he noticed Teddy starting to nod he turned the music down to a low buzz, just loud enough so he wouldn't have to drive in complete boredom. He has been mouthing lyrics, tapping his clutch foot in time, trying to stay awake. Poor Teddy, not because he keeps falling asleep, but because he keeps waking up. Adam can sense the cycle without taking his eyes off the road: First Teddy's chin will dip, then he'll start to undulate with the motion of the truck. He becomes a spineless dancer, one of those giant inflated figures condemned to dance outside used car lots, with nothing inside them except what is pumped in from below. Then he wakes up again. Adam can pinpoint the moment it happens, not because Teddy moves much or says anything, but from a kind of change in atmosphere, a sudden thickening of the space between them. It is the sound—except there is no sound—of somebody remembering what they have done. Poor Teddy, because imagine waking up over and over and each time that realization junking you in the face.

Adam should start watching for the turn-off he wants to take, onto an even smaller road. Once they're on that, they can pull off somewhere and he can sleep too. He has just enough energy left, the kind that comes from being relied upon. When he looks at Teddy asleep, he cannot decide what he wants to see. A good guy who went crazy for a few moments? Poor Teddy? Or the other thing? Over the next few kilometres, Adam's pity turns to a colder sort of curiosity, a desire to know how it must feel, then almost to envy, before it all finally ebbs away and exhaustion and boredom give him the urge to play. His discovery is that he can wake or half-wake Teddy by oh-so-lightly touching the brake, which pushes Teddy's limp body forward into the seat belt, causing his chin to rebound off his chest. Each time, Teddy surfaces without knowing what woke him, maybe without knowing that he slept at all. But each time he must be getting junked again, by a sense of doom that takes a moment to locate. Adam studies him out of the corner of his eye, and *studies* is the word: he wants to know how it feels. Teddy makes no effort to change position; he doesn't lean against the window or turn sideways in his seat. Occasionally he grunts, or sighs, or opens his eyes, but he never says anything. Each time, he must be remembering, going from innocent to guilty at the touch of a brake pedal. Adam does it a couple more times before his conscience catches up with him and tells him to change the game. From now on the goal will be the opposite: to drive smoothly, to take each turn as gently as he can, to keep Teddy unconscious for as long as possible. He counts in his head, and after he sets a record he waits for Teddy to drop off again so he can try to break it. The longer Adam can hold him under, the longer Teddy stays blameless, a good guy, poor Teddy. Adam keeps hoping that at some point Teddy will fall into a deeper sleep, and be unrousable, but it doesn't happen. Eventually he gets bored of the game, and of being alone, so turns the music up. Teddy wakes properly now, looks around with an expression like he's swallowed air and can't belch it, then drinks what must be the cold dregs of his gas station coffee. It's a long time before either of them speaks.

Up the smaller road, small enough that they would have to pull over for anything coming the other way, fatigue begins to eddy inside Adam. He wriggles his toes to stop the deadness creeping up his legs. He snorts like a horse because it feels nice. You should take a break, Teddy says. Adam says, We need miles behind us. Why? says Teddy. We're off the highway, what difference does it make? Poor Teddy. Dude, Adam says, are you serious? By now it'll all be out in the open. People will be reading about it. They'll be looking for us. A manhunt. Looking for *me*, Teddy says in a low voice. You didn't do anything. Okay sure, Adam says, so then I leave you by the side of the road? Teddy says, Maybe. Or maybe— But he doesn't finish. Adam counts to five in his head, letting the pause throb between them, then says, Maybe what? But Teddy, pussy that he is, just says, Forget it. They come around a long, slow turn, with the hill dropping away on Teddy's side. For a moment there's a nice view across the treetops. Adam says, Well, get the map out and find us a place where we can get clean at least. A river or something, small and out of the way. Teddy sighs as he flops the glovebox door and takes out the thick wad of map. They've given up on folding it properly now. It represents about a tenth of their country, covering Teddy's lap and the parking brake, stretching all the way to Adam's accelerator leg. Adam makes up his mind to drive them off it, into whatever is beyond. After a minute, Teddy says, Where are we? Adam takes his eyes off the road for a moment, his dark fingernail jogging the paper as he traces the driving he's done since the gas station. And just then, as if someone were watching them and deciding these things, something comes barrelling around the bend toward them. Jesus, Adam says, leaning back to his side. It turns out to be some kind of small bus, either for a tour group or some long-distance route. But neither of those makes sense out here, on this narrow road with weeds thick on each shoulder. What could there be to see? Where would anyone want to go to or from that would bring them this way? Both vehicles politely slow, ceding the centre of the road. The guy behind the wheel gives Adam a lazy wave. As Adam accelerates, a row of pale, bored faces pass, looking across into the truck without curiosity. Each one seeing, and perhaps remembering, Adam's scraggly beard, his black T-shirt logo, the black stripe that runs the length of the truck. What the hell are they doing out here? Adam says when the bus is out of sight. Teddy shifts in his seat, ignoring the map, which covers his knees like a blanket. He leans against his window and softly, so Adam can only just hear it, bumps his head against the glass, slowly, again and again. Adam wants to tell him to cut it out, but he is not sure he has the energy. Probably

Teddy is only doing it because he wants Adam to get angry. Probably Teddy needs someone to be mad at him right now. People invite anger as a way of absolving themselves for the other things they've done—the guy who cuts into your lane wants you to swear at him because he's having an affair and can ease his guilt with a counterfeit sense of having been punished. It doesn't matter who's doing the punishing, or why. Most humans, like ants, feel safer under a boot. Adam can't even remember where he heard that, or if it just came to him. After another kilometre he pulls over and snatches the map from Teddy, who barely reacts. Adam scans the ground they've covered. Little blue veins run through the area they're in, probably streams coursing down hillsides. He sees the hot springs Teddy wanted to go to, back on the main tourist route, the one they now have to avoid. Adam feels a sudden urge to swim, to be submerged. Then he sees a little heart-shape of blue to the west, with a dotted line leading toward it from the road. He calculates, then pushes the map back at Teddy and tells him to fold it properly.

The track takes them up a gentle rise, growing pale and sandy as the trees thin. Being off the asphalt is pleasant. Now Adam can feel the earth, its shape, even through tires, suspension, and sprung seat. There is a sense that they are about to arrive, as though this were where they had been heading the whole time. Teddy seems to have pushed the past day into a corner of himself. They talk about swimming, about how bad they smell. Adam imagines the feeling of cold water, the kind of water that stays on your skin even after you've stepped out and dried off, even once you're back in the truck and driving again. But after fifteen minutes the land falls into a wide, treeless depression, a near-perfect bowl, and a great carpet of ferns swamps the road. The blue on the map must just be whatever sodden ground is underneath. Either that or they have taken a wrong turn. Teddy wants to go back and try somewhere else, but Adam can see the track emerging again on the other side of the ferns; the curve of wheel ruts worn smooth is appealing for some reason, feminine, teasing its way up the far side of the depression and disappearing over a small rise into a cluster of pines. Plus there is some garbage or something off to one side, a colour that doesn't belong, so someone has been through here. Teddy gets out and walks to the place where the ferns begin, trampling one or two with his boot. When he comes back he shakes his head and says, It's pretty swampy. Get in, Adam says. When Teddy does, Adam grins and inches them into the ferns. Don't, Teddy says sharply, and is ignored. Adam stays in first the whole time, eyeing the opposite side and thinking at every moment the truck will stick or sink. He realizes he likes not knowing what the hell they would do if it did. About halfway across Adam can see silver flashes of water through the ferns, but there is no choice but to keep going. When the ground seems to finally firm up, Teddy says, Okay, well done, and Adam knows that even if there is nothing on this side, the trip across will have been worth it. In his side-view mirror he can see two perfect tracks of trampled greenery, the plants between the wheels having sprung back up unharmed, and water flooding the ruts. Water is always looking for a way. Adam imagines taking his clothes off and covering himself in mud, letting it cake dry before breaking out of the casing as somebody new. Teddy says, What now? I don't think this road goes anywhere. And Adam says, Would you shoot me? Teddy looks at him and then away. He makes a whining sound that turns into the word *what*. What do you mean? Of course not. He sounds like a kid when he says it, and Adam hates him for that. Teddy bites his fingers and coughs. Not like that, Adam says. I mean if we had to, if it came to it. If they had us surrounded. Teddy takes his hands from his mouth and squeezes them between his legs. Adam looks at the parallel lines in his side-view mirror, then forward to where the track bends out of sight. I guess we can sleep here for a bit, he says. Nobody's going to find us.

But he still wants to get the truck off the track, just in case. For all they know there might be airplanes scanning the area. Adam pulls into a narrow gap behind a stand of thick bushes, and he tucks the truck so well into them that Teddy can hardly get his door open. Branches scrape the metal when he tries. Under normal circumstances Adam would be worried about his beloved truck, but there's something liberating about the thought of it getting scratched up now. After making such a big deal about sleep, Teddy decides he wants to go for a walk. Adam wonders if Teddy is going to take the rifle with him, but he doesn't. Alone in the back of the truck, Adam smells his armpit, puts his hand into his underwear, smells his hand. There's a breeze outside, but inside it's still and hot; when he edges a window he immediately hears the drone of insects searching him out and quickly closes it again. He'll have to sweat. The acne on his back itches. He can see treetops moving in the wind, and the twigs and branches scrape the hood and sides of the truck in a way that makes his heart beat faster, though at first he does not know why.

Only when he finally closes his eyes, sprawling uncovered on his back with his legs spread wide, does he remember. It's the scraping sound, one of those childhood memories that has melded into his father's retelling of it. The sound of branches against the side of the house used to give him nightmares. The way Michael used to tell it, back when he still told stories like this one, Adam would appear beside his parents' bed, or blocking their line of sight from the red couch to the TV. He would be in tears, or close to it. The way his dad put it was *carrying on so much you couldn't make words.* When they calmed him down, he would say a bad man was trying to get in the house. This would sometimes happen twice or even three times in a night. They tried a night light, they tried moving Adam's bed to the other side of the room. His mom wanted to send him to a psychologist (Adam can hear the sneer in Michael's voice as he tells that part), but Michael solved the mystery before it came to that. It was as simple as a branch scraping the aluminum siding above Adam's window. What Adam definitely remembers is holding his mother's hand as they stood and watched his dad angle the ladder against the house and climb up, the red-handled saw in one hand. The saw was new back then, and it flashed like a sword, and his dad called down to Adam that he should come and hold the ladder. Six years old and his dad asked him to hold the ladder steady. He has imagined it to the point where it feels like a real memory: looking up at his father's strong calves, trying to keep the ladder still but in fact being rocked side to side himself by the motion of the saw. But according to Michael his mother had not let go of him, had called Michael insane for suggesting it, saying the thing would fall right on Adam's head if he stood there. So instead he must have stood with his mother's hands tight against him while his father wobbled there against the house, leaning dangerously out to run the saw back and forth across the branch. Adam opens his eyes to see the trees moving outside the truck; he may have fallen asleep just after he thought all this. He no longer knows whether it is memory when he sees sawdust catching the sun as it trails to the ground, waiting what seems like an age for the saw to break through and for the branch to come crashing down. It feels too obvious, like a shot from a movie. He is almost certain he has invented the moment when the ladder's feet slipped in the dirt, and his mother let go of him to run forward and grab it before his father fell. That is not in his father's version of the story. Perhaps it would be in his mother's. But he is sure about the sound the branch made as it dropped finally into the garden bed, and his dad smiling when he got down and saying, There you go, buddy, no more bad man. The branches are going to scratch Adam's paintwork. If it mattered, he would get up and move the truck. If it mattered, he would jump into the front seat right now and get the fuck before Teddy came back. He would throw the gun away and drive straight home to tell his dad or the cops or whoever. But then he and Teddy would have different stories, not a single one for them to share. And a story is what he needs. Teddy said Adam hadn't done anything back near the river. *You didn't do anything.* Adam feels bitter as he thinks, Not yet. He stretches, reaches an arm back between his shoulder blades, and scratches himself there until he is sure the skin is broken.

TEDDY HASN'T GONE far. He stays close enough that he will hear the engine start, both because he is afraid to hear it and is desperate to. Afraid to hear Adam driving away and desperate for the stillness that will replace him. It is due any moment. Even his feet seem to suspend themselves as they fall, waiting. Adam's face, since the shooting happened, has been cold and mistrustful as a parent's. Teddy puts two fingers from each hand into his mouth and chews, catching the smell of his breath and the sharp taste of bug spray—poison, though not poisonous enough. He wants to be abandoned, to deal with himself himself. He should have brought the rifle but could not think of an excuse. Taking it would have meant something; Teddy will never again be able to just do something and have it not mean anything. But at the same time he is sick of things meaning things, he understands now just how sick. Why these sudden paradoxes? They seem to cancel one another out, creating a teetering balance that any small misstep would cause to irredeemably collapse. He remembers her eyes again. The ring on her thumb. The pine needles here are springy underfoot, like the red stuff they put over the playground in town so kids won't break a bone when they fall.

But were kids breaking bones before? Teddy has never heard of it happening. Kids know the ground is hard, it isn't a difficult concept. The breeze hits Teddy's sweaty skin and cools it. He can hear flies, and when they grow quiet he knows they have settled on the damp back of his T-shirt. He bounces softly in his boots. There must be something else making the pine carpet so springy, moss underneath or something, not solid earth. He watches the woman's eyes as he bounces, gripping a trunk to steady himself; he brings his forehead to the bark and gives himself a dull bop, not hard enough to change anything. She knew what was going to happen before anyone else did, certainly before Teddy did. Teddy wasn't even aware he had fired until afterwards, when he heard birdsong rushing back into the void. Like when a cartoon character gets hit by an anvil or a boulder, that angry red finger of swelling, those cheerful birds neatly circling. Dollar signs ring up inside the coyote's eyes. When Teddy remembers the woman's grey-blue eyes, he knows they were telling him to face what was coming and be brave. They told him, though he didn't understand at the time, that things would work out one way or another. Now at least Teddy won't have to live like his numb parents, or Grace, who pretends her life will be different just because she's good at school. He won't have to worry about Ceecee anymore: he smiles to think she is on the brink of a miraculous escape. He can choose his trajectory now, aim himself at whatever he chooses and explode on impact. Bouncing aimlessly beside his tree, he tries to picture Ceecee but ends up thinking about his mother, who is easier to blame. The guilty sound of her keys hitting the dish when she comes home, the way she doesn't call out hello like she used to. She sneaks into her own house. Forty years old and having an affair with a bald accountant. Is that her way of escaping? Teddy has met him, and hated the fact there was nothing to hate about him. He had a plastic pen in his shirt pocket and told Teddy to call him Ron.

And then Teddy does hear it, the truck, and his mind is exquisitely empty again. The engine noise is the only thing inside him; his teeth almost vibrate with it. Teddy doesn't know what he wants but finds himself sprinting through the trees toward the sound, tearing off a short breath for every step. His boots thud against the forest floor, his heels hurt, the laces flail and click. He realizes he doesn't want to stop Adam, but only to watch him leave, to be there as the truck goes back through the dried-up lake and disappears down the track. He will listen until the engine sinks into the sounds of midges and birds and wind. Then he will be alone, his choices simpler. But it isn't like that: the engine shuts off before Teddy even glimpses the truck's black-and-red body. He slows to a trot for a last few steps, panting, and through the summer undergrowth he sees that Adam has only driven out of their hiding place, onto an open bit of ground beside the track. The suspension wobbles slightly, then the driver's door opens and Adam, in his underwear, walks to the tailgate and drags both their sleeping mats out onto the dirt. Teddy watches, unseen. Adam swats and slaps the back of his neck then stretches tall, holding a wrist with the other hand, armpits black against the pasty rest of him. He doesn't look around for Teddy—just piles the mats one on the other and lies chest-down on the ground. A moment later he is up again, leaning into the truck. He comes back with the bug spray, which he hisses onto his torso, arms, and feet. Finally, he squeezes his face closed and does his head. Coughing, he waves a palm in front of his face to clear the air. Teddy wants to laugh. He would laugh if Adam knew he was watching. But because he doesn't there is no point acting like an audience. Adam lies down again, a white body on a raft of sky-blue foam. Teddy watches awhile, waiting for Adam's body to move, and when it doesn't he turns and creeps back into the trees.

That evening they argue about a fire. Teddy says it will help keep mosquitoes away, but Adam believes the smoke will reveal their location. It won't be properly dark until eleven or even later. Eventually Teddy gives in, and Adam cracks a can of spaghetti and meatballs into the pot on the camp stove. Teddy puts a couple of chips in his mouth and sucks the salt from them. After getting one of their last full water bottles from the truck, he takes his T-shirt off and wets a corner of the fabric. When he notices the look Adam is giving him, he says, Aren't you sick of smelling like your own ass? But you can wet it down there, Adam says, pointing to the swamp they drove through. With mud, Teddy asks, disapproval in his voice. We've got to preserve the water, fuckhead, Adam says. Teddy says, Well whose idea was it to drain the water canister? Maybe it was the one of us who has some kind of plan, Adam says, his voice rising now. I'm only using a little bit, Teddy says, not quite obeying and not quite disobeying. He wipes his armpits before it occurs to him he should have done his face first—least to most filthy is the correct order, but it's too late now. He goes behind the truck to do his dick and balls and ass. God knows what he'll do with the T-shirt after this. He'll have to burn it. What he wants is a shower and a deep, clean, bugless sleep. He wants the two of them to be able to just pull into a motel. No, he wants to do that with Ceecee, to spend the whole night with her, which they have never quite done. Even when her parents went to a casino for the weekend and took her little brother with them, and she asked Teddy what they should do, smiling like they both already knew the answer. He remembers sitting beside her on his too-small bed, getting slightly hard just from the thought of it, and saying, I'm sure we'll think of something. Joking about it seemed like the adult thing to do, plus it was easier than imagining specifics. But after Ceecee went home that afternoon, nothing he could think to message her seemed meaningful enough. So they didn't talk much, and at school he found himself almost avoiding her. He didn't want to make plans in case he jinxed it; there were still so many days to go, so many ways it could go wrong. But with each school day the weekend loomed more and more, like a door through which there would be no returning. By Friday, on the fire escape where they all sat during lunch, she was cold, annoyed at him, leaning in close toward Brianna and saying things he couldn't hear. When he asked her about the weekend, Brianna snorted, and Ceecee said she didn't realize he still wanted to. Oh, I don't care, he said, I might be doing something with Adam anyway. Ceecee turned to Brianna. Right, she said. Of course. Teddy knew he should have said I don't *mind* instead of I don't *care* and that he shouldn't have brought Adam into it. The next day he told himself the only way to fix it was to just show up at her place like they'd planned. He stood showered and paralyzed in his bedroom, not knowing whether he was supposed to take things like a toothbrush and clean underwear. That would mean a bag, and a bag would make his parents or Grace ask questions. He never had to prepare when he stayed at Adam's place—they just passed out when they got tired or wasted. In the end he just put some condoms and his deodorant in his back pocket, stuffed extra underwear in the other pocket, and went off down the street. It was a long walk, and the farther he got the more embarrassed he felt. He needed to learn to drive. Something bugged him about the fact that Ceecee hadn't messaged him, that they hadn't spoken since Friday at lunch, and he found himself angry at her. He knew how easy it would be just to write, *You home? I'm on my way.* But why did he have to be the one? The overriding feeling, when the sound of an engine over his shoulder became Adam's truck passing and pulling to the curb, was relief. It felt only natural for Teddy to open the passenger door and get in. You need to get somewhere? Adam asked kindly. Yeah, Teddy said, but fucked if I know where. Then out of nowhere the day turned sweet: sitting side by side with Adam, driving, being driven, stretching his mouth around the words *girl trouble* and knowing they would fly like bullets over Adam's head. Suffocating, Teddy decided to say. Clingy. And Adam said, I know what you mean, man. Which he didn't, of course, but that made it even sweeter. Nobody wanted any more of Adam than they got, except Teddy himself. And being able to say with a sigh that things were not going well with his girlfriend, being able to hint that there were things about it

Adam wouldn't understand, was like winning the prize all over again. Buy one, get one free.

After they eat their canned spaghetti, Adam walks down the slope and crouches amid the mud and ferns. When he comes back his food bowl is brimming with brown muck and he says, See? Teddy laughs. So you'll smell like a swamp instead of an ass. You're the one who's going to have to sleep next to me, Adam says. He rests the tin bowl, which technically belongs to Elizabeth, on the hood of the truck. When he pulls his camo pants down, Teddy can't help noticing the fading bruise on his leg, a green-and-yellow smudge below the ragged hem of his boxers. It looks as though it used to be painful. How did you get that? he asks. Don't you remember? says Adam, wetting his T-shirt the same way Teddy did. You punched me. The day we left. I don't remember that, Teddy says, recognizing a note of regret in his voice. Look at it, Adam says proudly, smiling as he angles his leg and pulls the skin tight. Look, you really got me. You're not looking!

They do not speak while Adam washes himself behind the truck. Teddy listens to the sounds of Adam's body and the slosh of filthy water in his mother's camping bowl. The stars are beginning to come out. He fetches the bourbon from the glove box but doesn't open it. He rests it in the sandy soil in front of Adam's chair, to be waiting for him when he comes back.

Later, when they're lying side by side in the dark, Teddy sniffs the air and tries to laugh. Want to know what's funny? he asks. I smell like a swamp? says Adam. No, you smell like a mix of a swamp and fucking canned meatballs. The sound of Adam chuckling makes Teddy feel safer. And there's still a bit of ass in there too, he adds. Neither of them says anything more. Teddy blinks in the dark. He doesn't think he will be able to sleep, but he does.

ADAM CLIMBS A spongey rise and turns, making sure the truck is out of sight. The forest gets thicker the farther he goes, stems sprout low down on trunks as if the tree is too slow for them, they can't wait to get going. All this life, so sure of itself, determined to shoot its pollen or lay its eggs or whatever, before the silence and snow return in a few months' time. It is clear to him that hormones are just a trick, a way of keeping you in line. Nature has to literally drug you to make you want to have sex, otherwise why would you? It's another good reason to break the cycle, to avoid becoming his father or even either of his uncles, who at least have nice houses and take their kids skiing and sugar shacking but are still purveyors of the finest in fakeness. One day the kids will be the ones with kids, and nothing will have changed. Adam sees no reason to respect his cousins, except Cameron, who has at least a flicker of comprehension in his otherwise dull eyes. Cameron steals from the liquor store he works at. He changes the numbers in the system to make it look like certain bottles were never there. There is something exciting about that, the simplicity of changing a digit and hitting enter, the power to deprive something of ever having existed. As Adam walks, one of his hands lands below his belt buckle and squeezes lightly. His plan is to rid himself of the urge while Teddy is still asleep and he has the whole forest, the whole continent it seems, to himself. The sun is nearly above the trees; it's probably close to seven. This might be the longest he's ever gone without. Even before they did what they did, the fact of the road and never being alone meant Adam didn't get the urge, not even when he first woke up, which is usually when it's worst. This is far enough, he thinks. Teddy won't sleep much longer, and Adam needs a clear head with which to make decisions. He opens his pants enough to get his hand inside and conjures one of the scenarios he has stored inside himself. But it's too juvenile, and he discards it almost immediately. Then he has a stupid thought, a different sort of fantasy, that a bear will come upon him in the act and Teddy or whoever will find him mauled to death with his pants around his ankles. What a way to go, and he wouldn't be there to feel ashamed. The tree his other hand is resting on has a pleasing texture; he is vaguely aware of his thumbnail working doggedly into the bark. When Teddy's sister swung herself up from the couch that time, Adam saw up her skirt. But he can't really remember what he saw, which leaves only the fact that he has chosen to think about it at all, the fact that he stored it away with the rest of his collection, and the fact that thinking about Grace is just another way to fuck with Teddy. At least there is the body itself, the temperature disparity between his penis and his palm, the pleasure of holding and being held. He thinks about being tackled and cuffed, held down with his cheekbone in the dirt; he thinks about the smell of clean laundry, the time Elizabeth washed some of his clothes while he was at Teddy's house, how they came back smelling like they belonged to somebody else; he thinks about all the bodies he can remember, a faded and featureless parade; he does not think about the blonde he saw laughing on the side of the road, but that doesn't mean she isn't there. She keeps out of sight, watching him between the trees. See the boy, leaning forward so he won't spill semen on his pants or boots, hanging on for dear life. Adam, who will die a virgin, stands in the forest surrounded by dumb, indifferent organisms. A new patch of dappled light has begun to grow in the soil at his feet, tenacious sunlight piercing the foliage. The sun warms the sea, clouds rain over the land, rivers flow back to the sea. Trees turn carbon dioxide into oxygen. Adam needs a clear head. He is the one in charge. He flails, grasping at simulated acts he has watched and memorized, not settling on any individual but rejoicing in the collection as a whole, all the people who have become his private property. The thought of being a collector of women is enough to bring a great vacancy rushing into him; he leans helplessly against the steadying tree and mechanically empties himself, just barely enjoying it. Then he exhales and is businesslike, keen to forget every place his mind just went, reaching carefully for the water bottle that is still in his back pocket. While he washes he notices a dark spot on his naked thigh, which becomes a red smear when he smacks it. He smiles, to and at himself. He had forgotten about the mosquitoes. They have probably been feasting on him this whole time.

THEY STUFF QUARTERED oranges into their mouths with the rind facing out, giving themselves waxen grins that make talking impossible. They stand side by side, suckling the fruit and staring into the swamp that Adam brought them through the previous day. The tire tracks are now perfect parallel channels of black water and broken plant stems. One of Teddy's orange pieces is too big for him; he struggles to get his lips around it, juice and drool escaping. When he finally finishes he extracts the peel and kicks it neatly into the ferns, where it sets the water rippling in a wheel rut. He wipes his chin and sucks his fingers, eats another and kicks that away too. Then Adam joins in, kicking harder and more deliberately, sending his peel farther on a flatter arc. Teddy is exhausted by games, but even now it is as though he has no alternative. The sugar and acid are making his teeth scream. He swallows, rubbing a helpless tongue against furry enamel. When he tries to outmatch Adam's kick, his final piece of peel slices off his boot and skims through the dirt, coating itself as it rolls to a pathetic stop midway down the slope. Adam, who has a fresh piece in his mouth by now, lets out a nasal, demented laugh, and when Teddy looks over the toothless orange clown grin is like something from a horror movie.

Teddy assumes they will head back through the swamp to the road they were on yesterday, but Adam wants to keep going, to see where the track leads. It doesn't go anywhere, Teddy says. The line on the map stopped at the blue bit, remember? Adam says he doesn't trust the map, that a road always ends up at a place or why would it be there? What's the bet? says Teddy, but Adam just shrugs and leans to pick up the empty bourbon bottle. Adam looks like he's about to lob it into the ferns, or even smash it on the stony ground, but instead he opens the camper and stows it gently inside the folds of tarp. They can fill it with water when they find some, Teddy realizes. Adam is being smart. Then Adam tells Teddy he should drive this morning, to get some practice in. So that they can go twice as far. They shut their doors at exactly the same time, a thick and comforting beat. Teddy stares at the dash and the wheel and feels the pedals give beneath his feet. He tries to remember the things he has to remember. Before he turns the key he looks in the mirror at the bright green ferns, knowing they will be back here before long.

But Teddy is wrong, the track does lead somewhere. After they climb another hill they hit some old asphalt, and five minutes later there's a junction. Teddy stops, and they stare down each of their options. Adam carefully unfolds the map. So we aren't where we thought we were, Teddy says. Wait, Adam says, we can work out which way is north from the sun. Teddy, careful to keep the clutch compressed, watches doubtfully as Adam leans out his window. The morning sun is in no-man's land, between a ridge and the treetops of the valley. Does that make the ridge east, or does it just seem that way? Never Ever Smoke Weed, Adam says, twisting and gesturing the four points with his hands. So north would be . . . that way? Adam is pointing back the way they've come. What about this, Teddy says. We went north yesterday, then left off the highway, so that's west. So if we turn right . . . Adam swears at the map again. I mean, it's fifty-fifty, Teddy adds. Inside him is a submerged sense that none of this is going to matter. He eases the clutch out and, without any say-so from Adam, turns them right. Adam belches sour citrus into the space between them and fans it away with the map. Fun and games, he says.

Teddy has to concentrate; this is his first time driving on a proper road. At any moment Adam could yank him, tell him to pull over and get back in the passenger seat where he belongs. Out of the corner of his eye he sees Adam's thumb stroking his phone automatically, barely looking at the screen as he chooses the morning's music. You turned your phone on, Teddy says. Flight mode, Adam says distractedly. He puts on the German metal again. It's dark and enveloping, all the more comforting because the lyrics are incomprehensible, just a vague, all-purpose anger. A while ago, Adam, who lives on forums about this kind of thing, told Teddy what the album title meant, something like *Fortress Accident*, at least that was how Teddy remembered it. It wasn't accident, but something similar, a weird word, occident. Adam enjoyed explaining it, but it didn't seem like anything Teddy really needed to get his head around. Mostly it's nice having something to fill the silence of his concentration and a beat that prompts him to change gears. A gravel shoulder rolls past, between Adam and Teddy and the bright green things making the most of summer. In a few months, roads like this one will probably be under a few feet of snow, impassable. Anything on the ground will be lost until the following spring. But before then there will be men in snow-white suits and blue surgical masks, and yellow police tape, and gloved hands putting items into snap-lock bags. Teddy's DNA could even be in a lab by now. Tiny bits of Teddy in a test tube. A pipette. Drops of him suspended in liquid, then falling one by one. A dribble of Teddy in a petri dish. How weird that Adam is simply sitting beside him in the passenger seat, letting him drive while the pipette goes drip drip into the petri dish. He reaches a blind hand into the empty chip packet beside him, which crinkles like a baby tarpaulin. He slides his forefinger into the greasy corner where the ketchup flavouring is, brings it out, licks it, sticks it back in. This time the finger comes out bright as a blood test. The salt is glorious on his gums, and Teddy comes close to glimpsing how this will end, a swelling that feels a lot like love for his friend, like the brink of a great watery release, being able to piss when you were about to burst, knowing you can let go whenever you choose. What's funny? asks Adam. I just thought of something, Teddy says. Adam is waiting for him to keep talking, but he doesn't know exactly how to put this into words. Adam is the type of person who does research, who puts a German metal band's lyrics into a translator to find out what they mean, who has opinions, who believes things. What Teddy should say is that he understands Adam in a way he never did until now, until this exact moment.

It's just that we're driving down this road, Teddy says, and we're never going to come back here again, and that's okay. He thinks Adam will laugh, but Adam nods, saying with enthusiasm, You can't live until you realize you're dying. That's good, Teddy says. Is it from a movie? Adam shakes his head and says, My mind. Teddy remembers Adam's secret book of wisdom, his podcasts, and the channels he watches. He doesn't have any of that out here, unless he brought the book and is reading it secretly, when Teddy goes off to shit. Nice, he says to Adam. He puts his hand back in the chip bag and out comes a blood-red fingertip. Up ahead the trees are so green they're almost black, and through them a silver speck begins to grow, something reflecting the sun, a metallic or glass thing, a car coming toward them. Except it seems to stay in one spot as they approach, so it's more likely that somebody has pulled off to the side. Teddy has been doing so well with the clutch, but now he shifts down too soon and the truck lurches. Teddy swears. As he tries to compensate by giving it more gas, there is a noise of metal touching metal, something even Teddy can tell is bad. He wonders if Adam hears it too. But Adam's thoughts are somewhere else; he is sitting upright in the passenger seat, a worried furrow in his forehead. Keep driving, he says. I guess we can't stop and ask them where the hell we are, Teddy says. He sees Adam's white hand move to his door handle. Keep your speed and drive past, Adam says, like it's an order. The other car moves in and out of view through the trees as they go around a wide bend, then they pass it, a station wagon with roof racks, pulled off the road on Teddy's side. Even though he isn't positive, he says to Adam, There was someone

122

inside. The driver's seat was down flat and there was somebody in there, maybe asleep. Adam says, Keep going past those rocks, then pull over. He still has his hand on his handle, and as Teddy slows he cracks the door. Teddy moves onto the shoulder and lets the truck roll to a heavy stop. So what's the plan? he asks, words that sound stupid even as he says them. Teddy should know without having to ask, and in fact he does know. Adam is already outside. Just wait here, Teddy hears him say. Don't kill the engine.

But they are in enough trouble already. But they should be trying to get as far away as possible. But they will answer for what they have done and what they do from here on. Teddy tosses these objections up one by one, and one by one boots them away with the simple and unbeatable truth that nothing matters anymore, or more likely never did. The truck's rear slaps quietly closed, and Teddy searches the mirrors until he locates Adam walking from the shoulder toward the line of trees. His cap is pulled low like one of the marines in Patriot. He is creeping, almost dancing, as he moves toward the black car. As Adam closes the distance he hugs the trees, using the hunting stance they both know from the game. How unreal the reflected figure seems, its legs like the scissoring arms of a machine, the head barely rising or falling, rifle a diagonal protrusion, lowered but ready. Teddy is suddenly aware that this walk is something Adam must have practised. He thinks of the way Grace used to learn dance moves in her bedroom without even closing the door, and how he used to make fun of her, then get angry when she simply ignored him.

He makes sure the truck is in neutral, then gets out to watch Adam. The black car looks like it was once expensive. Teddy can only see its front half—the rest is blocked by the scrub and tall grass Adam is now stalking through, approaching as though he knows someone is inside. Teddy finds himself saying silently, again and again, that there isn't anyone there, that he was mistaken. Probably Adam will just check if the doors are locked, or shoot the tires, or put a bullet through the windshield to see what sort of pattern it makes. Everyone knows windshields don't shatter anymore: safety glass. Maybe Adam has forgotten that. Maybe Teddy should run and remind him of this elementary fact. The driver is probably off fishing, or hunting. Teddy takes two steps up the road then stops, his thighs tense. A hunter would have a weapon too. His stomach makes a noise, an internal fart, as Adam rounds the back of the car. He is definitely acting like he can see somebody. Teddy has heard that people who do a lot of driving will just pull over and nap whenever they get tired. Day, night, whenever. You lose all sense of time out on the road, somebody said once, either his own father or one from a movie, he cannot remember which.

The rifle rises a little more with each step Adam takes. He stops now, having looped around so he could approach the driver's side from behind. Adam is being smart. For a stupid moment Teddy tells himself that Adam has planned all of this, that Adam mind-fucked him somehow, that in fact it was Adam who shot the guy and the girl. That would make him Adam's hostage, a victim. But even thinking this is childish, because he remembers her eyes telling him to be brave. He remembers the sound, the *report*, which was always the word in the Western novels his dad pushed on him in middle school. You'll like these, Ted. Plenty of action. Even some saucy stuff. Adam is aiming now, Teddy wonders at whom. In Patriot you get more points for a headshot, plus it looks cooler. You can also buy hollow tips, but they're a waste of money, really. Fun once or twice, but the serious players like Adam and his gamer friends look down on them as toys. He remembers the gun jerking in his hands and Adam dragging him back to the truck, the sensation of having his own weight taken away from him. Teddy wants Adam to come back before it's too late. Probably the girl and the guy aren't even dead. Someone would have come along, the air ambulance chopper would have landed right there on the tarmac. He thinks of her lying on blinding hospital sheets, a tube in her nose, balloons, a fluffy toy from the gift store, *Get Well*. Teddy blinks and part of him very sincerely wishes them both all the best, as though they were just people he had read about in the news. And now Adam is trying to copy him. Copycat. Teddy once got called that for showing up to school with brand new sneakers the same as another kid's. A group of boys pulled his shoes off and they all spat together in the dirt, they made a communal pool of salivary mud and rubbed Teddy's sneakers in it. Was Adam one of those boys? Teddy cannot trust his memory but can see himself kneeling in the dirt, can hear the shrill, unbroken voice, one of a chorus. If Adam does this then the cops will be able to work out which way they're driving, their trajectory. But if he doesn't do it, whoever is in the car will tell the cops all about them. Or at least all about Adam, the man with the gun. Teddy sees police taping the scene off, roadblocks. There's been an incident, you'll have to go back. Armed and dangerous. ACTS PROVE. Cops looking for casings in grass just beginning to brown. School starts in five weeks. A forensics guy with a digital camera. Those snowy hooded coveralls Teddy is picturing are so the cops' DNA doesn't contaminate the important stuff. Teddy in a test tube. Adam once showed him a website that pays you for your jizz. But you have to be eighteen, and Teddy is just shy. His DNA is everywhere, though. Shiny casings in the thick grass. Teddy feels protective suddenly. He wants Adam to himself. He is sick of games but cannot help himself, and this one is easy. Then Adam will come back and they will keep driving. A cloud blocks the sun, and he turns away from his friend. He leans back into the truck and puts the firmest part of his palm on the centre of the steering wheel, where the horn is.

THERE WAS A particular moment when Adam first understood killing as something that could be done well or poorly, like anything else, like soccer or homework or the magic tricks from the how-to book he'd gotten for Christmas. He had been left, for some reason, at his grandmother's house for the weekend. As it was snowing, and because he didn't have his proper warm things, he wasn't allowed outside. Instead, he had been given control of the TV, to watch kids' shows until they gave way to whichever drab sport the public broadcaster could afford the rights for. Who knows where his mother and father were, or whether they were together or apart that weekend. His grandmother was in the kitchen; Adam could hear her percussive soundtrack accompanying his cartoons, a wooden spoon turning repeatedly in a metal bowl, cupboard doors clapping shut, the pop and hiss of the gas burner. Now, Adam has clearer memories of the sounds she made than of her herself. She seemed to always be in the next room, just out of sight beyond an open door. He remembers going to that house once more, after she had died, and how obvious it was just from listening to the empty rooms that she wasn't anywhere on earth anymore.

That morning Adam was watching one of the animations that bridged childhood and adolescence, featuring oddly ageless kids, usually orphaned, with spiked hair and a superpower. This one was about a boy-inventor whose best friend was a robot dog he'd made himself. Adam loved the depth of his grandmother's couch and its tobacco smell. He had learned to hold the nippled remote with one hand covering the end so he could fondle the buttons without changing anything. He was already old enough to find secret pleasure in the contrast of rigid plastic and soft rubber, and the odd distribution of weight, much heavier at one end, that meant it could balance on his palm in a way that seemed impossible.

As the show ended in a rush of credits, too fast for even a grown-up to read, Adam shifted, idly running his fingers across the buttons, waiting for what would come next. His covering hand must have moved, because he accidentally changed the channel. He tried pressing the number he wanted to get back to, and now found himself somewhere else entirely, as a bearded man with large hands explained something about soil. After that Adam didn't trust the numbers, so squeezed the down arrow and began a long descent back to the kids' shows. He caught a second of each channel on the way down, passing one anonymous face after another, news anchor, woman in purple coat, man shouting, man and woman really close like they would kiss . . . None of it interested him: he wanted to make it back before the next animation started. Until he landed on something that, for some reason, made him release the button. It must have been a rerun of something from the seventies. A man with a brown moustache, brown trousers, brown gloves, and a yellow sweater that crested beneath his chin was moving in a way that made Adam both excited and slightly afraid. The music was creepy but also the kind you could dance to. The man shuffled elaborately along the orange wall of a room, his shoes twisting in shaggy yellow carpet, his eyes twitching and rolling like he was mad. He *was* mad. After a moment Adam grasped that the man was not dancing but sneaking. He paused beside a door, and as the music tightened into a single, violinish shriek, the camera jerked upwards to reveal a painted portrait of the woman—Adam didn't know how he knew this, but somehow it was obvious—the man was about to murder. A close-up showed his gloved hands and the glint of something emerging from a pocket in the tight trousers. The moustache rose and fell with each breath the murderer took. This was the moment Adam stopped being afraid and understood he was watching something both unreal and beautiful. The man turned the door handle with a brown-gloved hand, inched the door open with a brown boot, and disappeared inside. The violins ceased, and for a moment there was nothing but an empty doorway and the faint sound of a woman singing within; it was the sound of somebody who believes she is alone, but she was not alone, because the murderer was in the room with her and Adam himself was just outside the door, waiting to be admitted. He waited and waited, until finally the cut came, silver wire around a pulsating throat, vivid fingernails grasping, eyes growing wide and then wider and then rolling theatrically away as all four hands relaxed as one, commanded by a new finality in the soundtrack, and even his grandmother's kitchen noises, so it seemed to Adam, grew still.

He is proud of himself for stalking so silently, for being professional, and with Teddy doubtless watching him. Before anything else this may be, it is a performance. He raises the rifle and tries to slow his breathing, though he does not succeed in unclenching his jaw or separating his tongue from his palate. The driver's seat is reclined, the man is on his back, a chubby face turned away from the window. He has swaddled himself with a quilted jacket and tucked his arms inside, leaving only the head visible. The bulk of him swells with each sleeping breath. This is different to whatever it was Teddy did. More professional, Adam believes. But anything worth doing requires both skill and will, the book says, with skill most often the easier to obtain. Adam has circled the car, assessed his surroundings, kept his ears and eyes open, his footfalls gentle. All it takes now is the will. He has already released the safety. He is perhaps two metres from the car window. Close enough. He imagines the rifle is an AR-15, and when he does that something strange happens, a tingle. He feels aware of each part of his body. Toes, fingers, even the crisp meeting of hair and scalp. And okay, yes, his junk too. But he feels utterly in control of himself. He does not think of the old movie he saw as a kid, or the countless times he has since played at shooting and killing. He is present in the world. He is everything he has been trying to teach himself to be.

The sleeping man has not been taking care of himself. If the car was not such a nice one, Adam might assume he was a vagrant. His beard is a wiry mess, with strands corkscrewing over his mouth. Otherwise he is nearly bald. Adam concentrates, but comes up against a wall. At first he cannot name the obstacle, but the creeping sense enters him that from where he is, Teddy may not be able to see him. So Adam scissors carefully through the gravel, keeping his eyes on the sleeping man's face, until he is standing in front of the car, aiming through the windshield. Adam repeats Teddy's words in his head, keeping his other eye open and his left hand relaxed. He roams the head before deciding on the chest. When his fingertip grazes the trigger, a rigid bolt enters him, something deeper and more significant than fear. The swaddled chest expands and contracts. Adam lets his finger curl. Fist-squeeze rather than finger-pull, Teddy said, all one motion, shoulder and hip firm but not locked. He concentrates, until his concentration is broken by the sound of the truck's horn blasting over his shoulder. For a moment he is wild, startled, unsure whether to turn around or not. Maybe there is danger coming, maybe he needs to run for the trees, maybe Teddy is just trying to fuck with him. He jerks his head, but there is nothing to see except the visible portion of his truck on the shoulder, taillights pale in the sunshine, Teddy's ass as he leans inside the driver's door. Perhaps Adam looks a fraction too long; by the time he turns back to the job at hand a man's soft face is staring at him, eyes big and mouth trying to process. The eyes and the mouth are both saying *holy fuck*. And while Adam is still trying to get his head clear enough to raise the rifle again, the pudgy face stops processing and the man puts his hands in front of his face to catch the bullet. Light skims off the windshield. If Adam was going to shoot he would shoot now, but he stands dumbly, listening to the little grains of gravel collapsing beneath his boots, the muffled cry from inside the car, and that fucking horn, still blasting. Perhaps Teddy just wants to make this a little harder. After all, he hit a moving target. How many times, while lying in his bed or driving the dull streets of his town has Adam reminded himself to always be ready, to have his will on hand when it's needed? When Teddy finally kills the horn, Adam can hear the man's raspy scream more clearly. The man's hands are groping for the keys and his jacket slides down to reveal a rounded belly in a faded polo shirt. Adam still cannot seem to do anything. He is betrayed. Even the gun is lowering now, deflating in his arms. There are two men in the scene, but neither of them now is Adam: he has become a mere spectator, wondering if the man in the car will manage to escape the man with the gun.

The engine starts, the black car lurches and stalls. The fact of Teddy's betrayal finally brings Adam to himself. Teddy is being selfish, and it is as much a case of not letting Teddy win as not letting the man get away. Nudged by this injustice, he raises the gun again and brings his hips forward into a posture of authority. He can see himself in the man's eyes, a figure surely too young to be holding a gun that way, or to have that immovable look on his face. Adam smiles, inwardly at least. He has forced the man to choose between committing his own act of violence by running Adam down or nestling into victimhood, knowing he could have saved himself if only he had had the will. So Adam gets to be a spectator after all, waiting to see what happens. In flashes he thinks of how suddenly Teddy started firing back by the river, how it came out of nowhere, how he got the girl through the neck and how unreal that looked, a wonder of nature, how neither of them has talked about the fact that they both just watched in fascination for a few seconds as the blood came out in great generous gulps, how for a minute they were just two boys again, staring the way you stare at a movie, their mouths slit open at the lips. Get out, Adam says, too quietly for the driver to hear. He gestures with the rifle, taking a step back so the sun isn't reflecting in his face so much.

Who knows what the man in the car thinks of, whether he summons people he cares about or who rely on him, or conjures anger to give him strength, or whether it is as simple as adrenaline squirting blindly from its gland. Whatever it is, he calls Adam's bluff, manages to start the car again and guns straight for him. The driver does not even steer for the vacant gap of road that slivers open as Adam hesitates and shifts aside, but right at the boy, as though the only route to safety were between his legs. Adam, beaten, finds himself lunging, dropping the rifle. The car swings onto the road toward Adam's truck, then brakes with a brief squeal. The driver, the man, even has time to sweep a wide turn before he speeds off in the opposite direction, the one Teddy and Adam came from.

Adam has gone cold. As he walks back to the truck, he knows he will shoot Teddy here and now. He will not say a single word but shoot him, and then there will be no more distractions, no more negotiations. Adam will own everything, will run the table. He can imagine the before and after, the feeling of destroying something meaningful, of having tested himself and passed. But as he covers the fifty metres between him and his final decision, the certainty falters. Teddy is watching him from the driver's side window, his spine submissively curved, head down, eyes up. Adam responds by unconsciously moving his own shoulders back and slowing his steps, making Teddy wait for judgment. Teddy doesn't seem especially afraid that Adam is walking toward him with a gun. He looks ready to be punished, like he wants it. As Adam closes the distance between them, another plan begins to form, a smarter way to resolve this.

NOTHING CHANGES. THE same greens and greys flood the windshield, there is the same tension of Adam's accelerator foot half pressed down. Teddy, back in the passenger seat, watches his fingers caress the door's catch, as though at any moment he might find himself pulling it and hurling himself shoulderwards from the moving truck. He imagines it further: rolling, burning wet grazes on his hands, his hips, his face, skin sloughed so easily away; wondering if bones are broken, knowing he cannot lie there in the road but must get up and reach the trees before Adam has time to react. Time to get up, pal. Teddy, time to get up. His father's voice. And the sound of the truck first idling then dying. Opening and closing, the driver's door and the tailgate. Adam's coaxing voice, Fun and games. The bloody taste you get from your chest when you can't run any more but you run anyway.

When Adam got back to the truck, all he said was, He's gone. To which Teddy could only nod. Adam put the weapon away, not under the tarp anymore but on top for anyone to see. Then he indicated with a flick of his hand that he would drive. It must have been the fear of standing face to face with Adam, of them having to step around each other, that made Teddy scoot his bottom over the parking brake and centre console instead of getting out and walking around like a normal person. Then Teddy shrank into his seat, waiting to see what his punishment would be. There was a slowness to Adam's movements as he sat behind the wheel, making a show of adjusting the rear-view. Teddy watched the little dark hairs that petered out on Adam's knuckles, the way the pink left his hands as he gripped the wheel. The keys, Adam said then. Huh? asked Teddy. They're not in the ignition, Adam said, and put his hand palm-up between them, not impatient exactly, but waiting. Teddy had pocketed the keys unconsciously, though he could not even remember turning the engine off. When he handed them over, Adam said thank you in a weirdly formal way that sent a ripple of fear through Teddy. The thought surfaced then that he was out here, in the middle of nowhere, with a stranger. With nothing to do but wait until Adam decided they had reached their destination.

Now they have been driving for five minutes, and Adam hasn't said anything more. The longer things go on, the more Teddy squirms. He rubs the butts of his palms into his eyes until they water and burn. He blinks at each white dash that comes toward them. Adam is taking them in the same direction as before, not following the man who got away. God knows whether they're going north or south or whether that even matters now. When Teddy pressed the horn it felt as though a great rush had swept him up and he had no say in where it would take him. It was simply the only thing to do. He thought he would be able to explain it to Adam in a sentence, but Teddy can barely find any words at all. And now there is silence, he has broken something. Teddy wants to take his punishment and be refreshed, like in games where it's better to die and start over than to struggle on depleted.

The boys, or men, have become unstable. For Adam it is about equality. Nothing is more important. Teddy is robbing him of something, which is unjust. Teddy knows this, too, and in order to make it up to Adam he places himself prone, inviting retribution, opening his legs for a kick to the balls. When he can't bear the waiting anymore, he says into the silence, Did I fuck up? Adam replies straight away, as though he has been waiting for Teddy to make the first move. You just got scared, Adam says. Don't worry about it. Then Adam does maybe the most fucked up thing he could do to Teddy: he reaches beyond the hand-brake and pats Teddy's leg once, twice. Teddy was bracing for something very different. He thought he was prepared for what would come. But now an unspeakable panic rises in him: Adam is going to keep making him wait. The kick to the balls will come, but not now while he's bracing for it. Sometime later. They drive on in silence like that, like parent and child, disappointment on one side, fear on the other, and between them a bolt ready to be slid home.

ADAM STARTS TO feel something when he puts his foot down. More like a lack of something. He is exhausted, wired on Monster and potato chips, and his first thought is, Teddy has broken my truck. Teddy with his clutch-crunching and his thudding his head against the window and his disgusting crusted feet on my goddamn dash. He has no respect for other people's stuff. Adam glances over but does not say anything, yet. For a few kilometres he can believe he imagined the engine problem. He drops into fourth and tries accelerating again, and he does get more response that way, for a time. But then fourth starts to feel like fifth. Teddy asks why they're slowing down, and Adam doesn't reply. They are once again in a thickly wooded place with needle-straight firs hemming the road, blind curves, glimpses of dense nothing on either side. The hill they are ascending is gentle, but Adam can tell the truck is struggling slightly. Doing eighty instead of a hundred makes the outside world more real, less like images rolling by and more like an actual place. Adam notices the constellation of insects that have pelted the windshield in the last five days. He notices trees and soil and asphalt, things that will be here long after the truck has passed out of sight. He tells himself the hill must be steeper than it looks. But then a gentle shudder moves through his foot from the gas pedal. He drops into third and is comforted by the torque, if that's the right word. It makes the seat hug his butt more snugly. He loves his truck, he trusts it in a way he trusts few people, and for the first time he can imagine it failing him, leaving them stranded beside some unknown bit of highway, sitting ducks, just like the couple in the hippie van were.

Once, long before he ever learned to drive, Adam saw a bumper sticker that read TORQUE DIRTY TO ME and thought it was the coolest, even though he didn't know exactly what torque was. He knew it basically meant power, the thing he is losing now. Of course he dutifully checked tires and oil before they left, the way Michael taught him to. It can't all be Teddy's fault. The truck is keeping secrets from him. What's up, Teddy says again, and Adam has to admit that he doesn't know. It doesn't feel right, he says. It doesn't sound right. Did it feel weird when you were driving? Teddy shrugs helplessly and says, I don't know what it's *supposed* to feel like. Adam decides that blame is exactly what Teddy craves, which is why it should be withheld. Anyway, the clutch doesn't seem like the problem. Maybe the engine's overheating after so many continuous miles. Between them they've gone almost non-stop since they found their way back to the right road. There are no warning lights on the dash, but Adam isn't sure where the temperature gauge is supposed to sit. He remembers his dad telling him that the needle pointing at cold is just as bad as it showing too hot because it means the thermostat is screwed. He could stop and check the oil, but they don't have any extra with them, so what good would that do? He has been focusing on the need to escape at the expense of all else, including what happens after escape. When Adam imagines standing on the hot asphalt with the hood up and midges clouding his head, he feels panic and a tension in his wrists. They would have to flag somebody down. Adam would have to make amends for his earlier failure. He wonders if the cops have by now warned drivers not to stop along this stretch of highway. If nobody stopped, if he were alone with Teddy, could he still prove himself?

Hoping for a distraction from what he thinks is a new, throaty note in the sound of the engine, he flicks on the radio. The static is a comfort, proof that at least they're alone out here. Still, he scans the whole dial for a station, saying to Teddy, I want to see if they're talking about us. Adam himself does not know if this is a joke, a provocation, an imputation, or something else, but it calms him to say it. He likes that Teddy has no answer. Teddy is doing the thing where he punches himself in the leg without realizing it. Adam thinks of the bruise on his own thigh, which he can now only barely feel. At the end of the AM dial is a fuzzy country song, violins and a woman's voice. It plays through a verse and a chorus, but more and more static washes into it and when Adam eventually reaches to turn it off a red light begins glowing on the dash. Listen, he says into the silence. We need another car. How, Teddy says, angling himself away from Adam's side of the truck. I mean, Adam says, we don't have a choice. Teddy nods, and Adam can tell his friend is begging to be told what to do. A change of plan, a new mission, a short deviation from the inevitable. All Adam has to be is resolute. He likes that word—it's what the American presidents' desk is called. It reminds him of the picture he put in his locker back in January, just to fuck with people, and how he and Teddy had a bet on who would be the first to complain about it to a teacher. Idiots. And that same week, Mr Coomb wanted them to debate immigration but then told Adam he couldn't say that the illegal who raped a girl was illegal, that he couldn't use either word. And yet somehow Adam was the one being told he was ignorant. But facts are facts, aren't they? he had said, genuinely surprised. When school starts back, the two of them will be the subject of a special assembly, and at this thought a smile tightens his chest. There will be no doubt in anybody's mind which of them was in control, which of them was responsible. Does Adam wish Teddy were more his equal, or does he enjoy being depended on, knowing he can steer Teddy the way he does the truck? When Adam first had the idea to leave without telling his dad, he didn't think he would actually do it. It was just something to think about, a fantasy to make staying seem less depressing. It was only when he knew Teddy would be with him that it stopped being a fantasy. He needed someone in the passenger seat or he would never have made it this far.

Wild ideas rush by like debris in white water: What would his first move be if he saw flashing lights in the rear-view? How quickly could he reach the rifle? Can you really get shot just by reaching into your pocket, pretending you have something in there? And what if he got hit some place that didn't kill him? He remembers what he said to Brianna Vicci months ago, about being visited in jail, and he swallows at the thought of having to watch his dad cry again, a pathetic, shaking Michael across the table from him, just like on the never-ending nights after his mom escaped. Only this time Adam's chair would be bolted to the floor; there would be no angling it away. Like those tables they installed in the park beside the marina, the ones people picnic at, acting as if they live somewhere nice even though the bay is polluted to hell and stinks at low tide, and the men are all either broken like Michael or pretending like Teddy's dad. Teddy's mother told Adam to call her Elizabeth. From what Teddy has said, she is on the cusp of escape too. Maybe we stop and let it cool down, Teddy says out of nowhere. Maybe it needs a little water. It sounds like something you would say about a horse, a living thing that can be restored through rest, food, love. Adam says, You know if we stop there's a chance it won't start again. That'd suck, replies Teddy, on whom nothing ever seems to dawn.

As they head down the other side of a rise, Adam shifts into neutral and coasts. The warning light fades away. The sky ahead is clear and blue; there is even a heat shimmer on the road. What a summer, though, Adam says, and even he is aware that it sounds like something he has picked up from an older man, like when a child uses a big word out of the blue. And then they're climbing again, and the truck is struggling in third. The temperature gauge has inched up and the engine sounds choked, like it needs to cough something up. When Adam puts his foot down he feels the shudder again. Is that a turnout? says Teddy. Should we stop? It's coming up on Teddy's side, a gap in the pines along the shoulder, an exit to a new situation. Suddenly, a motorcycle comes out of nowhere behind them, swinging wide around the truck.

It's one of those enormous travelling ones, with a windshield and metal cases on the sides. The rider's helmet is open-faced, and Adam watches a chin turning briefly to show itself in profile. Adam has already taken his foot off the gas, preparing to turn off the road; the rider thinks the gesture was for him and puts a hand up in thanks as he accelerates into the distance. You don't see that very often, says Adam. See what? says Teddy. A Black biker. How do you know he was Black? Are you blind, says Adam, didn't you see? See what? says Teddy. This is Adam, drawing lines in the dirt simply to make his friend choose which side to stand on; and this is Teddy, smart enough to play dumb. They have slowed almost to a stop by now, and with the motorbike out of sight Adam eases them into the turnout, the suspension jostling him, making him ill. He does a neat three-point turn so they're facing the road again, idles, hesitates. How do we steal a car without anyone noticing? asks Teddy then, and Adam wonders if he is in some kind of denial. Adam's answer is to turn the engine off. Fun and games, he says into the silence. I guess now we'll see.

Outside is the sun-whitened world, screaming cicadas, and an ominous syncopated ticking coming from the engine. Even the hood is way too hot. Adam pulls off his T-shirt to use like an oven mitt and hoists the metal up onto its stand. He hardly knows what he is looking at, a network of tubes and cylinders, things beyond his experience. It smells like plastic just about to burn. Only check the oil when the engine is cool, he remembers Michael telling him. He pours water into his palm and lets a drop hit the metal. It sizzles and is gone. He wipes the rest into his face and leans against his door, not looking at Teddy, who is still in the passenger seat with his seat belt on. Through the camper window Adam sees their mess, the half-folded tarpaulin, unrolled and scuffed sleeping mats, empty bottles, the twin canisters, red and blue. It looks just like Adam's bedroom, teenage and inconsequential, except for the rifle. Without saying a word to Teddy, Adam takes it out and checks it over. If the truck doesn't start, it will be all they have. Teddy finally emerges, and Adam feels watched as he tidies up. He puts the gun away beneath the tarpaulin, rolls up the sleeping mats, decants dregs of water into a single soda bottle. A car flashes by on the road, and they wait.

Without turning on their phones there is no way to sense time except by the gradual cooling of the engine. Neither of them talks for a while. Teddy puts his boots on and takes the toilet paper and goes off into the woods. Adam hovers his hands inside the hood now and then, until the engine is cool enough to tap with the pads of his fingers. He plucks a maple leaf and uses it to wipe the dipstick. There is something there, at least, some amount of oil. Or maybe that's worse because it means the problem is more serious than low oil. Adam circles the truck five times, thinking, then once in the other direction, for luck, as Teddy emerges from the trees. He comes up to Adam with the toilet paper tucked beneath his arm and his hands cupped, asking Adam to pour some water into them. Gross, Adam says, but he does it. Teddy rubs them against each other, unsoaped, then wipes them on his pants.

Back inside the truck Teddy makes a sort of giggle and says, Moment of truth. Adam shuts his door. The key is still where he left it in the ignition, the key to his father's house hanging limply from the fob. It does not occur to him that he might fear being alone more than anything else, or that he has little sense of himself except as reflected in others. What would either of them be without the other to define him? Adam would rather be nothing than be alone by the side of the road or sweating in the woods as he walked farther into nowhere, though facts like that are kept packed away most of the time. If they weren't, he wouldn't be able to function. Nobody would. He puts the clutch in and pulls the stick into neutral. With Teddy beside him he can handle the unformed and looming thing that is approaching them. Even if it had to happen right here, on this blazing afternoon, he would do it. He puts his foot on the brake, turns the key, and the engine, of course, starts.

WHAT A SUMMER, though. The weather holds for longer than it usually does this far north; plants and insects get a few extra weeks' furious emission, the birds have more to eat, everybody has more of one another to eat. First local, then national outlets begin to gush trauma. Such violence, they stress, is unthinkable. But the story is another matter: the story is a commodity in demand. People want to know what happened and what happens next. Trip of a lifetime, tragedy struck, in broad daylight, senseless killing, police say, perpetrator or perpetrators, fled the scene, remains a mystery: the bloodier a story, the easier to tell it in ninety seconds or four hundred words. The script already exists; it needs only minor alterations, as well as a map from the graphics department to show people how close to or far from fate they were. Pictures of the victims are sought out, cropped, enlarged. They show two people smilingly alive, oblivious to the eyes now on them. And it is this as much as the crime that makes them so tragically, so unbearably, innocent: the fact that they do not know they are being watched. Their story is told over and over, slightly differently each time. It is *developing*, which means it is ripening, straining the stem, getting ready to drop. It means the danger has not passed. It means: don't look away. Act two brings relief, a minor victory, the reluctant hero who shrugs beside his wife, interviewed on his own lawn chair in his own yard. When the reporter asks what he was thinking when it happened, his inevitable answer is that he didn't think, he just acted, and that is what saved him. Over staged video of the man getting into his now-famous car, the voice-over returns with a final platitude and the descending cadence of the sign-off, then it's back to the studio for an update, the breathless word MANHUNT on the lower-third strap, the script read live to incorporate the very latest. The story takes its curves at speed. Those watching can ask *How could this happen?* without ever having to answer. There is no time to answer. There is the constant promise of the new: new threads and plotlines and unexpected turns, hourly updates, a twisting road that may suddenly and without warning arrive at its terminus. A loose association of amateurs begins studying satellite images, theorizing and speculating. They do this out of a desire to have been instrumental, to have been right where others were wrong, to claim their place in the story. They also do it because it is a fun game to play. Among them are those who guess the truth before the police do, winning them admiration and status. They are the happy ones. The officials hesitate, knowing instinctively that these missing boys are more likely to be victims than perpetrators. They have urged drivers not to stop on three stretches of highway, a triangle of sorts, though there are not enough resources to effectively enforce or even communicate this; there are plenty whom the message does not reach. On a warm evening, one of the unaccounted-for boys stands beside a road and flags down another driver, asking if he has any spare oil. The driver says he does not. The boy looks uncertain, in fact vulnerable, so the older man offers to inspect the boy's truck and even to extract some oil from his own tank to share, though he does not know how exactly this would be done. When he expresses surprise that the boy is alone, the boy says that his cousin is with him, that his cousin became angry about breaking down and went off into the woods an hour ago and has not come back. The driver sees fear in the boy's eyes and decides it is not only the result of engine trouble. The driver explains that he does not know much about engines, wanting to keep the boy's expectations in check, though the same desire to have been instrumental makes him lean confidently into the truck's open hood and gently touch the different parts as he locates the dipstick. The boy is standing uncomfortably close; he smells as if he has not changed his clothes in a while, a sweet mix of fecal and body odours made milder by the breeze. The man smiles, feeling a surge of fondness either for the boy standing beside him or the boy he himself once was. Then, after he extracts the dipstick and turns, he sees the teenager backing slowly away through knee-high grass, toward the line of trees. There is no particular expression on the boy's face now: not fear, concentration, hatred, or amusement. It looks perfectly blank. The man is unnerved by this behaviour but turns away from it; he is focused on the problem he has been tasked with solving and the satisfaction that awaits him if he succeeds.

*

The real reason Teddy never learned to drive: by the time it was time, his parents frightened him. Teddy didn't want to be in an enclosed space with either of them for any length of time, with no possible escape, in case it turned out to be the day his father finally broke or, which would be worse, his mother confided in him. Getting a licence was independence that required utter dependence to achieve. So he adapted, walking farther, and making friends with Adam, who was happy to drive Teddy around in exchange for minor tributes. If Teddy had only accepted his sister's offer to teach him, he would never have let Adam get so close.

The Toyota sedan is silver and automatic. That's why Adam says Teddy should be the one to drive it, because it will be easier, even though Teddy would be much more comfortable in the truck. They need to find a secluded place so they can pack everything into the new vehicle and dispose of the truck. Adam says they will burn it. Teddy's arms are rigid on the steering wheel. He is trying not to breathe too deeply, so he won't have to inhale the car's human smell. He waits for the truck's taillights to illuminate, waits for Adam to take the lead. He wants to put the window down but doesn't know how and cannot take his eyes off the truck. Over and over, his mind plays notes from the racing game he grew up on, the sound that signifies the final lap. After an absurdly long time, Adam starts up and Teddy puts his foot on the accelerator and follows. This is the first time he drives alone, with no one guiding or assessing him. He could go anywhere, he thinks—that is the whole point of driving, isn't it? He could turn in the other direction and try to lose Adam. He could reach a good speed and aim for a tree. But neither of those options seems any more productive than concentrating, following the truck back onto the road, and letting Adam's taillights guide him.

WHAT'S A MORE definitive way to possess something than to destroy it? In some part of himself, Adam has been preparing for this since the beginning, not just since he and Teddy set out but since the morning he bought the truck with a thousand embarrassed bucks of accumulated birthday cash, mostly from his grandmother, all his McDonald's savings and the rest from his dad. When he brought it home he deliberately blocked Michael's car in, just so he would be called on to move it again when his dad went to work that evening. It felt like a grown-up thing to be asked to do. He did a lap of the vehicle in the driveway, tracing the broad stripe that interrupted the blood-red body halfway up the doors. Adam felt sure he would never know anything so beautiful, an extended-bed with an Ultrix camper on top, enough to get two people clean across a continent. Never mind the fact that nobody on this continent would want to go on a road trip with Adam. He'd have plenty of room to stretch out. As soon as Michael had left for work, he'd found the spare comforter and put it together with one of his pillows and a towel in the camper. That way he could always leave if he needed to, and being able to leave made staying more bearable. Ever since that day, he has been driving toward this one.

Fittingly, he is alone for this final trip, which is partly what reminds him of the day he bought the truck. He can see Teddy in the rear-view, making panicky little *S* shapes in the Toyota, a sign that he's focusing too close on the road just in front of him, worrying too much, overcorrecting his mistakes. Best not let him drive too far on his own.

In fact, the first place Adam tries is perfect: a fire-scarred turning circle littered with cans, and a widish sandy track that leads farther into the trees, hooking until it's out of sight. Teddy pulls in awkwardly behind him. He's done well, all things considered. They both get out, quickly confer, then get to work. Teddy seems glad to have an uncomplicated task; there is a shuffling obedience to him now, as though what they just did had broken the last remaining strand of something in him. Adam feels energized. He bundles armfuls of sleeping mats, loose clothes, and grocery bags into the Toyota, moving as though working against a clock, which of course he is. He puzzles a solution for the two gas canisters, which won't fit in the trunk so have to go in the footwells behind the front seats. Together, they pile up their remaining food and scant water. There's a carpet bag already in the Toyota's trunk, which neither of them touches. What was the fuel gauge doing? asks Adam as they work. Teddy stops, looking at him cluelessly. The gas, Adam says. I'm asking you how much fuel is in the Toyota. Oh, Teddy says, and leans into the driver's side to look. Adam has just picked up the rifle from the Toyota's back seat to reorganize the space. He walks toward Teddy and readies a laugh: he knows what's coming. Oh shit, Teddy calls out, it's empty. Teddy straightens when he hears Adam laughing at him, bumping the back of his head on the door frame. Adam laughs harder and hands Teddy his rifle. What's funny? says Teddy. Adam says, You have to turn the ignition on, dummy. Power on, gauge works. Now Teddy has to laugh, too, because at this moment, *dummy* is a term of endearment, an I-love-you-despite-the-fact. Well how the fuck was I supposed to know, he says. I never drove 'til like yesterday. You drove great, Adam says. He sits down right where the dead man was sitting less than an hour ago. He turns the key and watches the needle rise. It reaches a third, two-thirds, nearly three-quarters. How much is in there? asks Teddy. He's holding the rifle in two hands like he's a golf caddy, waiting to offer it back to Adam. It's as good as full, Adam replies. We could siphon some from the truck, Teddy says. I've seen it done. Adam has seen it done, too, on television, but he wouldn't know how to do it without getting a mouthful of gas. You need a pipe for that, Adam says. Like a garden hose or something. We don't have one. I've thought of that, says Teddy, brightening suddenly. We can use the one from under the hood of the truck. After we get the truck in position we won't need to move it anymore. Adam says, The more gas we leave in the truck, the harder it'll be to identify. He doesn't like the idea of raping his truck for parts. It would be disrespectful. When he got his driver's licence they made him say whether he would willingly donate his organs to save a life. He'd written HELL NO in block letters on the form.

Once they finish shifting their belongings, Adam does a final check and sees, beneath the passenger seat, Teddy's phone. He reaches in, then pulls his hand back. If Teddy won't look after his own property then it's his loss, says a part of Adam. Another part wonders what Teddy might do if he switched it on and got reception. When he closes the door, Teddy is leaning against the tailgate, hands in his pockets and a foot kicking the dirt. It makes him look like a shifty character from old T v. *What now?* says the look on Teddy's face. Reload the rifle, Adam tells him, in case anybody comes. We have to wait until it's properly dark.

They tacitly agree to spend some time alone, each free to wander through the trees with their thoughts, take a shit, jerk off, whatever. Adam follows a slope until he finds a shallow stream, and thinks about taking his boots and socks off to stand in it. He watches mosquitoes alight on his sleeves and pants, slapping them one by one and flicking their bodies into the air. He scoops a double handful of water and wets his hair, combing it with his fingers. He thinks he might be getting bitten right through his clothes. When he walks back he spots Teddy across the clearing and they nod to each other like they're strangers, hikers passing on a trail. The sun is dipping, and Adam can tell himself that he feels at peace, both with Teddy and with what they are doing. There is a good deal of right in it. Finally, they find themselves back in the bare truck, slumped side by side on reclined seats. The last of the sun angles through the trees, and Teddy slaps the visor down on his side, then opens the map and says, I want to go to these hot springs. That's where I wanted to go in the first place. Adam is on the verge of telling him not to be stupid, that they can't let themselves be seen, but something about the prospect of doing something so normal feels exciting, legendary even. How will the fools of the world ever make sense of Adam when they find out he did what he did and then went for a swim? He imagines himself entering the ranks of men who are despised, remembered. Sure, he says. Let's just not get lost again. I mean it, Teddy says, I want to go there if it's the last thing we do. The line is cliché, but Adam wonders about it, and about what Teddy thinks is going to happen from here on in. Okay, Adam says. I'm saying okay. He gets the last of the bourbon from his backpack and they sit in the truck and drink like they've done countless times before. They talk about the basketball team they both like despite its being located two thousand kilometres from where they live. They talk about school, using the past tense in a way that might simply refer to the year just gone. Teddy tries to tease Adam for landing in detention so much, and Adam finds himself talking about punishment, saying what the book says, which is that the purpose of punishment is neither deterrence nor rehabilitation but simply to make the victim feel like they are not alone in their victimhood. It makes warped twins out of victim and perpetrator. But with detention there is no victim, Teddy says. Not usually. It's just because you broke some rule. Adam doesn't say anything to that. He is thinking, trying to piece some things together. Weird question, says Teddy, sounding tipsy. Did you ever get hit? I mean spanked? He says the word *spanked* softly, as though he is unnerved by it. Adam laughs through his nose. What? No. You freak. Fuck off, Teddy says quickly, I mean as punishment. Like by your parents, when you were little. Adam says, Are you about to tell me you were? Teddy looks glad to have been asked. Yeah, my mom did, he says. Never my dad. I only remember it happening a few times. I must have been pretty young, five or six. Adam's thoughts go to his own life at five and six, finding nothing he wants to share. Teddy says, I remember my mom stopped doing it after a while, because I figured out how to make it hurt her more than it hurt me. Adam watches him flex his face in a weird way, scratching his chin in long, slow movements. That kind of punishment always seemed so terrible, Teddy goes on. But at some point you realize that it doesn't actually hurt, that it means nothing. I worked out that all I had to do was squeeze my ass cheeks together, I mean clench—here Adam starts laughing—and then it didn't hurt at all. And the best part is my mom got mad that I wasn't crying so she tried to hit me harder. Teddy is on the verge of laughing, too, but holding it together so he can keep telling the story. She hit me so hard she ended up bruising her own hand. Seriously. A day later it was all blue. She showed my dad and I thought he was going to go completely ape at me, but he just laughed. He was on my side. And after that she never did it again. Both boys are chuckling now, Teddy with the giggle he only uses when he really can't help himself, Adam with his mouth closed, forcing it all out his nose. But soon Adam has had enough of laughing and takes a swig of bourbon to silence himself. So what did you do? says Adam after he swallows. What did you do wrong in the first place, I mean, to deserve it? Who knows, Teddy says. I honestly don't remember. I used to fuck around with Grace a lot, like hide her toys and make her beg me for them back. I wasn't a very good brother,

I guess. You stole her dolls? asks Adam, ready to pounce, but Teddy doesn't take the bait. And if he doesn't take the bait, there's no point. Yeah, Teddy says, either her dolls or this tambourine thing she loved. I think I ended up breaking that.

When Teddy goes out to piss Adam looks into the sunset with his eyes closed, watching his eyelids wash with red and black. Something Teddy said has made him feel afraid. He doesn't know which bit exactly, or what the fear is, but he knows that if they don't keep moving, he will sink into another layer of himself and will never be able to claw his way back up. Not having done it would not change anything in the long run, he tells himself. He has to remember that, and trust it. He should have brought the book. Just having it around makes him feel safer, less alone. It is a father to which he can defer. The bits he so carefully memorized, that he copied into a notebook as if they were diary entries, are beginning to blur in his mind. Thank god for Teddy, to talk to, to teach, to be better than. Adam thinks about what he would do if he were alone right now, about how he didn't have the guts to shoot the first time, and how different it felt when they were in it together, a team. He was doing it for Teddy. Through the windshield he sees his friend only a few metres away, swaying slightly from the bourbon, looking up at the sky. There's a hint of green cloud at the horizon. They have come so far. Maybe they can make it to the Arctic after all. He wants to be with Teddy a little more before they have to stop, to drive north, to take him to the hot springs he won't shut up about. Adam starts the engine and drives farther into the trees, edging down into a little gully that runs toward the stream he found earlier. It's quite a slope and the truck falters, begins to slip sideways. For a moment Adam believes it will roll, and feels the thrill of not wearing his seat belt. But the truck rights itself at the last moment and slumps, crushing brush and ferns, nose first into the ditch. With the angle, Teddy's phone has slid forward from under the seat, and Adam leans to pick it up. He climbs out and walks back toward where he can see Teddy's dancing headlamp.

Teddy's light goes out before Adam reaches it, and a moment later they nearly walk right into each other in the dusk. Jesus, you scared me to death, Adam says. Teddy smells bad. He turns the headlamp back on, laughing like an idiot and blinding Adam. Then he shines it at the outline of the truck. Wait, you can't do it there, Teddy says. What do you mean? asks Adam. Forest fires, Teddy says. There are trees right above it. You were supposed to go over there, onto the sandy bit. Well it's not moving now, Adam says. Where's the lighter? If we start a fucking wildfire . . . Teddy begins, but Adam jumps in: Then no one would find the truck. Or, actually, they'd think we died in the fire too. Give me the lighter.

Adam feeds one of Teddy's stinking T-shirts into the gas tank, draws it half out again. The air grows rich with the smell. Fuel is nothing but potential, after all. They learned that in science class. He holds the T-shirt for Teddy to light, then they step back and watch the fire work its way into the gas tank. Adam is in awe of the modest flame, which seems only to grow smaller and less significant. But Teddy puts an arm out and ushers Adam back. Perhaps he senses that things will change quickly and without warning. The bloom shrinks until it is not much more than the glow of whatever is smouldering down in the tank, sending out tentative fingers now and again. Then it roars, comes back with a vengeance, and they are shielding their faces from a spurt of orange flame. Adam turns and sees their shadows stretching lengthily away. They step back again. The paint buckles. Trusty steed, Adam says, wanting it to sound like a joke, but it isn't. Teddy says, Oh god, it's going to catch that tree there. But he's wrong. A few branches crackle briefly into flame, but it does not spread. They've been watching the truck burn for a couple of minutes when Teddy says, Shouldn't we go? Anybody could see the fire from the road. Adam is thinking of a witches' sabbath, the story they read in English where the guy's wife begs him not to go into the woods at night because there's evil there, but it turns out she just didn't want him to find out she was going there herself to fuck Satan in a clearing. Does this story have a moral, and if so, what? the teacher asked them. Adam thought: And if so, so what. He wonders if Teddy would be Satan in this situation, making Adam do all of these things without seeming to. Teddy plays dumb but he's got an evil streak for sure. The way he just put a bullet in that girl. Fuck. And she was pretty, beautiful in fact. Maybe the most beautiful girl Adam had seen. All those rings that caught the sunlight. Her hair. Adam should strangle Teddy for that. Adam was just messing with the two of them, nothing more. He fingers the playing card in his pocket and for the barest moment he makes believe that the girl was his, Adam's girl, that Teddy killed her because he was jealous. Adam turns to look at his friend with such fierceness that Teddy says, What? The fire is raging now. Paint, plastic, metal, gasoline. A smell he could bite into. He can see the seats burning inside. It feels cleansing. Apart from Teddy, the truck is the last part of his old life. Its skeleton has lost all colour now, camper lost amid the acrid smoke and the flames. Something, a tire, sets off like a gunshot. Teddy turns, leaving Adam standing there for an amount of time he can't gauge. Eventually, Teddy shouts, using Adam's name, which normally he never does. Adam. Adam. Come the fuck.

When they're settled in the Toyota, Adam says, Here, I forgot. You left this in the truck. Oh, thanks man, Teddy says, taking the dead phone with an expression on his face like he wouldn't have minded much if it had burned. He considers it in his palm for a moment, then gets out of the car again and throws it as high and as far as he can into the trees.

THE TURNOUTS HAVE long begun to seem the same, like the landscape in older video games—trees and rocks placed differently, a puddle or a patch of darker green either present or absent, but with the unmistakable sense that any variation occurs on a uniform grid. The tape goes scrawk as Adam measures off a strip. Teddy has stopped watching him and stands with his toes apart, heels together, hands on hips, hair in his eyes, staring. Trees curtain them on three sides. Some distance away a rig roars past, its baritone engine building and fading with impeccable smoothness, a perfect parabola. The sun is bright, dappled through the pines, but Teddy realizes he is cold. He looks again at Adam, who has his X-Acto knife in his mouth like a pirate and is lining up a strip of the black tape he bought the day Teddy bought his rifle. His plan is to put twin lines down the centre of the car, which will, he says, disguise it. Teddy thought it was a stupid idea but has to admit that, from this distance at least, he is fooled. There is a little wind in the pines. A bird says the same thing over and over, and Teddy cups a bicep in each hand. The sound of another engine grows in the distance, but thinner, a car this time. He turns and looks toward the sliver of visible road. Adam stops what he's doing. Suddenly there are multiple cars speeding north, one after the other, a convoy. Five or six go by before the noise fades. Teddy glances at Adam, who is holding the knife dumbly in mid-air, his mouth slit open and tongue between his teeth. Teddy can't be sure, but from the little that was visible, the cars all looked white. He sees now that the police have simply been waiting for Adam to join him in his guilt. Now that parity has been achieved, they are ready for their punishment. The echo dies away and Teddy breathes, but the panic is still there in his blood. Scrawk goes Adam with the tape again, sticking doggedly to his plan. Teddy walks into the pines, feeling safer the farther he is from the road, from the stolen car, and from Adam. Adam once told Teddy that the only true difference between men and women was the way they responded to being alone. He has told Teddy a lot of things that seem trashy but maybe sort of smart. Teddy knows one thing: asking yourself what you believe the whole time is utterly exhausting. It makes him want to curl up, which is why he keeps fantasizing about driving to the nearest motel, clicking the lock, and sleeping in clean sheets. Either that or submerging himself in water. He no longer wants to go home.

When Teddy gets back to the car, Adam is still doing his thing. He suspects Adam just wants something to do, to feel that he is active in their situation, rather than how Teddy feels, which is like being swept down rapids with successive rocks narrowly missing his head. Adam has left the trunk open, and Teddy notices the carpet bag. He leans in and quietly unzips it. Where was the guy going? Where would he be now if it hadn't been for Adam's plan? There is a plastic folder with pages of printed tables and charts, and some neat shirts that Teddy instinctively assumes were folded by a woman. There are a few pairs of weirdly long socks, a sweater, a rain jacket, shoes without laces, and some smaller things that Teddy doesn't touch. He feels around the other side and hits on a smooth leathery thing, a pouch, heavy. Its zipper opens with an expensive soundlessness. It's a digital camera. Teddy doesn't know why anyone would have a digital camera instead of just using their phone, but then again they never found a phone. The camera makes an optimistic sound when he turns it on, loud enough that he looks up to see if Adam heard it. The navigation is awkward but Teddy figures it out and finds the videos that are stored on the camera. He clicks on the first one. The guy must be standing in the woods and turning slowly around, panning past fir trunks, light flaring in and out. Then the guy stops and zooms in on some rocks on the ground, then at his shoes, the shoes Teddy just saw in the carpet bag. And that's it. Video over. Weird. He goes to the next one. The guy's filming a camp stove with a pan of water on it. Teddy can hear the hiss. It's just that: fifteen seconds of him aiming the camera at a stove, the water not quite bubbling. There is no sign of who he is or why he is making videos. Teddy watches the opening seconds of a few more, part of him hoping for something dirty. There's a crackle from the camera's shitty built-in speaker, a combination of wind and birds and sometimes traffic. Hey, Adam says from the front of the car, come check out what I've done. Teddy doesn't answer. He wants to be alone with this guy for just a little longer. He flips back and chooses another video from the bottom of the list, which must be the most recent. This time the guy is by the highway; Teddy can hear but not see a car going past. The picture zooms in, and Teddy tries to see what the dead man is showing him. Then a voice, through the bad speaker, says: Would you look at that. A shudder hits Teddy at being spoken to, but he keeps watching. He cannot see what he is supposed to be seeing on the screen. He cups it to keep more sunlight out. The guy is zooming in and out, the camera shaking. The voice goes, Wowee. Check. It. Out. Isn't that beautiful? Teddy thinks, Who is he talking to? Then the shaky zoom goes close enough for Teddy to spot, swimmingly, a black bear on its hind legs. It's standing right by the road, looking across the lanes. The camera shakes as the guy steps closer. He says, The damn thing looks like it's waiting for a bus, Alina. Is that beautiful or what? The camera zooms out, and the voice says, Don't worry, honey, this is how far away I am. Then it zooms back in. Teddy is oddly gripped, and suddenly disappointed that he and Adam haven't seen a bear this whole time. The guy steps shakily closer, and the picture gets clearer. Oh my god, he says. One after the other, three awkward little cubs pop out of the bushes and follow their mother across the road. On the other side, the mother turns and looks right at the camera, right at Teddy. The voice moans, then says, Alina, would you get a load of this? I wish you were here. She's got *cubs*, Honey. She's got *three beautiful black cubs, my darling*, these last words coming in a whisper, right into the camera's microphone. There is nothing else, no more words. The bears walk into the shrubs, and once they are out of sight the video stops.

When Adam asks him what he has found, Teddy doesn't try to hide it. He offers the camera and says it's full of weird videos of trees and one of bears. But he does not mention the voice, or the things it said or to whom, and he is glad when Adam doesn't seem interested.

Later, when it is Teddy's turn to drive and Adam has fallen asleep, he thinks about the name Alina, wondering where it comes from. It's a pretty name, prettier than Ceecee or Elizabeth or Grace. Probably she is just some middle-aged lady, the guy's wife. None of it seems real. He keeps imagining Alina, and pretty soon he even has a face for her, which is basically the sad and serious face of the woman on the poster that has hung all year on their geography classroom wall.

HOW HIGH AND small the sun is—a coin burning through the clouds only to dash itself on the Toyota's window tinting. As he takes a curve, Adam watches his left wrist turn bluish green. He keeps right as cars and trucks pass on the left, more than they have seen in days. This is a two-lane road, the outskirts of a town. The fuel needle is somewhere between a quarter and nothing. The plan is to go just far enough into town to find a gas station, fill up, then get the fuck. He looks over at the passenger seat, a shifting rectangle of light on the grey upholstery. He's spent so much of the last year driving alone, but in this car the empty seat is an odd image, almost threatening. He indicates, pulls in behind a rig, then swings through two oncoming lanes to reach the gas station. Even as he's doing it he's unsure whether it's legal to cross two lanes like that, but there, it's done. Now the challenge is to buy just the right amount of gas and food with the remaining cash. It never occurs to Adam that he might attempt to rob a place like this. He doesn't want money; money would only have to be spent. He wants gas and food. He wants time. He could fill up and then tear away without paying, the easier kind of robbery, but what would be the point? Anyway, a place like this will have cameras. He keeps going back to a feeling of being observed. This morning, he opened his eyes to see Teddy watching the video of the bears again. When Adam came back from shitting, Teddy was still staring at the camera's screen, holding it as though he might have been filming Adam emerging from the trees.

He pulls alongside the pump, then realizes he is on the wrong side for the gas cap. He is nervous, maybe more so than he was for any of the other stuff. Maybe being in a town around people makes a difference. Witnesses, spectators, an audience. He will need to act in the other sense, the sense of make-believe. He only vaguely senses the main cause of his nervousness, which is the fact that Teddy could cry out at any moment, or start banging, or even accidentally kick against the trunk. If Teddy were discovered, it would be easy enough for him to play the hostage. He might even do it well enough to find his way back to school, to Ceecee, and to his parents. Teddy was almost too willing to get in the trunk when Adam suggested it, which made him very slightly suspicious. But it had to be done if they were going to get gas, they agreed—the cops would be looking for two. And Adam's place was clearly in the driver's seat. Teddy only asked Adam to buy fresh batteries for his headlamp, which is growing dim, leaving them only the Toyota's headlights and the flash on the digital camera. But batteries are too expensive. They need gas and food. They need time, not light. Thinking about it in those terms makes what he has to do now feel important, even epic, which of course it is.

Adam steps onto the oil-stained concrete and unclips the nozzle from its holster, trying not to look up at wherever the surveillance camera will be. An eye, watching them move across the country, an eye connected to a body, a body crouched and ready to spring. If he is so sure Teddy has been filming him, why doesn't he just take the camera and check? Because Teddy has claimed it for his own. The rifle, if anything, feels more like Adam's property now—Teddy has lost interest in it—but the camera is something Teddy covets. He keeps it in the pocket where his phone used to be, keeps watching those eerie videos the dead man made. He has it with him in the trunk right now, lying there in the dark. The gun is there, too, rolled up in the tarpaulin. Get some gum, Teddy had called out after Adam locked him in, and buy yourself a toothbrush, and don't forget batteries for the headlamp. Teddy will not be able to get out until Adam pops the button. What if he simply left Teddy on a side street and walked away? If he wasn't buying this gas, he would have enough money for something else, a bus ticket or who knows what. What if he drove back out into nowhere and did something even worse than walking away? Imagining it gives him a little rush of vertigo, oddly calming, because imagining it is reassurance he will never do it. He stops pumping and opens his wallet to re-count the cash. He can probably spend another fifteen on gas and still have enough for food. Behind the bills is the playing card, the one he took from the hippie couple.

On his way inside he subtly, so he thinks, presses down his little black tape stripe, which is already beginning to peel from the hood, a combination of the rain they had earlier and the relentless rush of highway air. It may not last much longer, but it does not need to. The moment he's inside the store he looks up to see a staring camera. Right back down goes the head, down like he's been caught out, hands go monk-like into his hoodie pouch, then come out again, swinging, unsure. That there is no one else in the store and nobody behind the counter only makes him feel more watched. He forces himself to walk, picking up bread, cheese, and a watery package of hot dogs. There doesn't seem much point getting anything healthier than that. There's sure as shit no point spending six dollars on a toothbrush. He glances at some newspapers in a rack beside the candy; if he looked inside them he would see himself, his name, photos. He would see an imploring quote from his father, whom he would hardly believe could be so eloquent, saying he knows that his son carries pain in his heart, and has done for a long time, for which he, Michael, can only blame himself, and then urging his son to come home while in the very same sentence admitting he is sure Adam never will. But the papers are stacked thick, their front pages obscured below the masthead, and Adam does not touch them.

There is a barrier between Adam and the young woman who has finally taken her place behind the register, safety glass or Plexiglas that tells of late-night armed robbery, ski mask and gun. The idea of a stick-up seems childish to Adam, who once tied one of his grandmother's silk scarves across his face for a game of cops and robbers and who now crouches awkwardly beneath the woman at the counter, trying to locate Teddy's preferred flavour of gum. His other purchases are piled up on his side of the screen, and the attendant waits for him to push them through the opening so she can scan them. And the gas too? she asks. Hi, says Adam, too brightly. Yeah. He rises with the gum in his hand. The woman is wearing a faded short-sleeved polo shirt with the gas station logo right on her breast. On the other one is a weathered plastic badge that says *Kara*. He keeps her waiting now, as she did to him, scanning for Skittles, walking back to the fridge for an energy drink. The urge to get out of here is held in place by the sense that this chance will not come again. He can buy whatever he likes. The woman is not bothered by the delay; she stares down at the counter where her phone is doubtless concealed.

Most of the items she rings in without touching, using the pistol-style scanner to edge them back toward the window for Adam to retrieve. He doesn't ask for a plastic bag, and she doesn't offer one. When she finally looks at his face, she hesitates. Where ya headed? she says while waiting to be handed the cash. North, Adam says with a straight face. The Arctic, actually. I got a job. Oh yeah? she says vaguely, looking past him at the Toyota, as if wondering how a car like that is going to survive that far north. Or maybe she has no idea what the roads there are like, or about what cars can and cannot do. Maybe she can smell how unwashed Adam is and his disgusting mouth, even from beyond the security screen. Good luck with that, she says, taking the last of their money. But now Adam has tasted the airy freedom of his lie and can see how easy it is to keep painting layers. Almost to his surprise, he finds himself making his fantasy smaller rather than bigger. Actually it's only a job offer, he says. I'll find out for sure when I get there. But I think it'll work out. He no longer feels childish or afraid. He wants to keep talking. He wants to keep Teddy waiting and wondering in the suffocating dark. He remembers a video in which a man argues that beauty should be mistrusted, especially in women. It acted on you in ways you were not always aware of and could not easily control. Thanks, Kara, he says deliberately when he gets his change. What? she asks. Kara, he repeats, then stupidly: Your name. She has put the money on the counter in a way that makes it impossible for their hands to touch. Oh, she says, with half a laugh. That's not my name. They make us wear a name badge, but we all just use this one. You want the receipt? Adam nods. What about if it's a guy working? he asks then. She has her answer ready, as though she has had this conversation more times than she has wanted to. The guys who work here don't have a problem wearing their name badges. Briefly, Adam is reminded of his old shame, the feeling of being worthless before somebody he finds attractive, the thing he has spent years working to defeat. He has also felt it with Grace, and a couple of the girls from school. It sparks a fresh desire to leave, to release Teddy from confinement and push on, just the two of them. Without saying anything else he turns away. He carries the loaf of bread in his hand; everything else is a bulge in the pouch of his hoodie.

When he gets back to the car he opens his wallet once more, takes out the playing card, and leaves it neatly on top of the pump, for the girl or somebody else to find. He imagines her trying to scramble her memories of him back once it becomes clear who he was, regretting not having paid more attention. But nobody finds the card. Sometime later the wind takes it, and it ends up in a puddle by the propane canisters, where it remains until the year's first snow and long after that, as the boys' names and faces fade from newspapers, from news sites, television, and radio, retreating into fissures of the internet where men, mostly men, divine and debate their motives, defend and damn them, or use them as evidence while arguing a crucial point.

TEDDY IS NOT stupid. His mind has passed over the same possibilities that Adam's has, and more. His confinement tells a story, or would do if there were someone to tell it to. He and Adam are witnesses to each other, not yet to anybody from the outside, except the guy Adam snuck up on, the one sleeping in his car. The one Teddy saved. If the trunk opened now and a shocked face stared down at his filthy, fetal body, it would not be hard to perform being rescued. He probably wouldn't even have to say anything: the story would tell itself. Miracle boy plucked from murderer's clutches. And yet, being bumped along in the dark like this, he feels safer and more comfortable than he has in days. The anticipation of emergence, of finally breathing clear air instead of his own stink, is comforting. The longer he remains in the cocoon, the more transformed he can expect to be. So why not stay longer? Forever, even. The road and its contradictions. He might have called for help when he sensed Adam was inside the gas station, after the pump and the spewing fuel had fallen silent. He might have felt around for some sort of catch that would release him—he is pretty sure modern cars do not allow you to just lock somebody in this way. But these things would have been nothing more or less than pranks, acts of mischief that try and fail to articulate the larger, unspoken thing. He can hear other engines around the car now, things going past, high- and low-pitched sounds giving a sense of vehicle size. Above him, a cold curve of metal protrudes into his space, one of the arms on which the trunk door levers up and down. It reaches nearly to his face. Teddy is reminded of all the nights he spent on the too-small couch in Adam's bedroom, how one end was overhung by a shelf that would threaten his head if he slept in that direction, which he mostly did, because the other way felt too much like he was sleeping at Adam's feet, like he was a dog or something. When the car turns sharply, Teddy's skull is squeezed against the carpeted metal and he presses his hands against it to ease the pressure. They must be back on the two-lane road now, but he can still hear other cars occasionally. There would still be time. He can see the scene from another driver's perspective: up ahead a trunk suddenly shoots open, and horribly, comically, a man throws himself into the road. The driver would slam on the brakes and come up just short, the air filling with the smell of rubber, the Toyota accelerating into the distance. This injured man would blink and try to move, try to roll onto his stomach and crawl. The driver would tell him to keep still, not to worry. Teddy would be told that he was safe now, that whatever his nightmare had been, it was over. During this fantasy Teddy's hands almost unconsciously begin to stroke their way around his perimeter. He imagines never seeing or speaking to Adam ever again, which is when he knows he has pushed the fantasy into the ridiculous. The carpeted surface is scratchy against Teddy's lower back where his T-shirt has ridden up, and he can smell his entire bouquet, from breath to armpits to ass crack, all harmonizing in the dark. Even before any of this happened, he was angling for the safety of the cocoon, or womb. And Adam is the only one who can tear him out of it. It will be Adam's face that he sees looking down at him, those small eyes and the smile Teddy still isn't sure he's learned to decipher, even now.

Does he fear the opposite, that Adam might abandon him? The answer to that would be another question, whether a child fears being abandoned by its parent, a dog by its owner. The answer is: constantly, but without ever truly believing it will happen. Fear from the perspective of safety, a game one plays with oneself for reasons that remain unclear until much later, provided later ever comes. How you doing, he hears Adam's thick and distant voice calling. How *is* Teddy doing? Adam promised him batteries if he got into the trunk, the way a kid is dangled a treat to make it do something it doesn't want to. Usually it's in the kid's best interests, though. Teddy's rewards are waiting. Adam has also agreed that they will go to the hot springs. He wonders if he would suffocate in here, given the chance. Adam will not release him until they reach a quiet enough place. Then he will get his batteries and his gum. They will eat whatever Adam bought, lie down side by side once more, and sleep. Five minutes pass before Adam calls to him again; Teddy enjoys not answering. Let him do his own imagining, let him think Teddy's lungs are full of carbon monoxide, let him think he is now alone in the world. The other engines Teddy could hear are now gone, and he feels like he could sleep if he tried. Perhaps he really isn't getting enough air. When the road gets bumpier, Teddy can assume it is a quiet one, some unpaved track leading them into the nowhere of the forest. Or else Adam has pulled two wheels onto a rough shoulder just to mess with Teddy, to jostle him. They seem to be driving faster now, as if Adam were worried. Still, Teddy reserves the right to say nothing, at least until he emerges back into daylight, fresh and new. That's what it will be like at the springs. When baby animals are born, and their mothers are licking the goop off them, they never look surprised about where they are. They just accept it. Teddy doesn't want to answer Adam or put his mind at ease. He is the one making the sacrifice, the one holding the cards.

TAKE YOUR TRASH WITH YOU, say five moon-white words on a squat wooden sign. In the appropriate place, someone has scratched the word FUCKING, energetically underlined. The trailhead looks like a place that usually throngs, but there is nobody and nothing here now. One of Adam's conditions was that they come in the short hours of darkness. The other was that they keep the rifle with them and be prepared to use it. He glides into the easiest spot, illuminating the sign about the trash and an information board next to it. Wait, he tells Teddy, who is already opening his door. Let me turn around so we're facing to leave. Teddy obediently shuts his door again, impatient. Adam doesn't know why, but he cuts the headlights for this last manoeuvre, using only the vague nocturnal glow and the reverse lights to guide him. Back at the turning, they passed a silent campsite and RV park, trucks and cars spooned around tents and cabins, all sound asleep except for a softly lit something, likely a block of restrooms. As soon as they wake up, Adam thinks, those people will make their way here, to swim and make memories, to experience nature's majesty or whatever. The Toyota's radioactive clock display puts them just beyond 2:00 a.m., darkish for another couple of hours. What they should be doing is using that time to get farther away, but Adam has found exhaustion beginning to unravel his thoughts, not necessarily in an unpleasant way. He tries to dig a thumb into the bruise on his thigh, but it's gone now; there is no trace of the pain he has grown used to checking in with. The silence thickens when he turns the engine off. Teddy, who was so antsy a moment ago, now puts his foot on the dash and relaces a boot incredibly slowly, focusing like he's only just learned how to do it. If this were the truck Adam would be annoyed at him putting his boots up like that, but there is liberation in this new sense of impermanence, as though they have broken through a membrane beyond which acts, not objects, prove who they are. Adam steps into the chilly air and opens the rear door. He puts two water bottles, one full and one empty, into his black backpack. He pops the trunk and takes out the cigar-roll of tarpaulin, leaning it against the car. The plastic bag with the ammunition goes into his backpack too. He checks the pockets of his jacket for the sunglasses he bought back at the gun store. He'll need them tomorrow, he thinks, when the sun is lashing down and they are far from here. He rolls his sleeping mat, attaches it to the bottom of his backpack, and, lastly, stuffs his sleeping bag inside. Teddy is not with him on these preparations but is standing beside the car, leaning on his open door, staring at a tiny moon. You good? says Adam, quietly. When Teddy takes his eyes off the sky his voice is innocent and much too loud: You're taking all that stuff with you? It looks like there's only one way in and out, Adam says. We need to be prepared if we can't make it back to the car. Teddy only shrugs, slinging his towel over his shoulder and reaching back onto the passenger seat for the digital camera he is never now without. Adam collects the bug spray and they perform the little rite they began a few nights ago, each one standing shirtless with arms wide and eyes shut, letting the other spray him down.

According to the information board, the springs are fifteen minutes down the trail. They take it creepingly at first, with only the camera's light to guide them. After a few minutes Teddy freezes on the track and illuminates a big thing, a bison probably, a dozen metres away. The light is not strong enough; they can only really see its outline. It seems to have scooped out a bed in the long grass and sits grimly, trying to decide if it is being disturbed. Fuck, Adam whispers, genuinely awed. It is impossibly big, the crest of its body like a distant hillside in the grey light. When it turns its head, curved horns join the silhouette. There are more of them back there, Teddy says, waving the light excitedly. Adam remembers the woods on their first morning, how Teddy shot at and missed the hares. A gunshot has a particular smell, which he hadn't known until then. There is a great nasal sigh, and Adam can tell the animal is disgusted by him. The rifle in his arms is still wrapped in tarpaulin. Firing it this close to that RV park would be a bad idea, anyway. The animal keeps staring as it slowly hauls itself to its feet, then it slumps farther into the trees, not making as much noise as Adam would have thought. He can't get over its size, that tumorous hunchback, the rolling confidence of its haunches. It moves like it's annoyed rather than frightened, like it wants nothing to do with them. Jesus, are those its balls? laughs Teddy. What a simple masculinity that would be,

Adam thinks, to be free of guilt and reason, to focus on nothing more than the creation of more bison. Animals have it so easy, Teddy says, as though he has read Adam's mind.

A bit farther on begins a boardwalk that leads through dead trunks, some erect and some fallen, across what seems like stagnant water. Adam looks at the moon and the pale sky and feels uneasy. There is a neat carpet of chicken wire nailed to the boards. Their four boots make ominous knocking sounds. God, I can't wait to get clean, Teddy says. The idiot has only brought a towel with him. We'll have to be quick, Adam says. Yeah, yeah, Teddy says, as though Adam were being overly cautious. In their hometown, Teddy comes across like a stunted Jesus, polite to adults and better looking than Adam, no zits to speak of. He doesn't know why that should matter anymore, but it does. The light from the camera is swinging with the movement of Teddy's arm, and occasionally Adam sees flashes of what's in front of them on the little screen. It illuminates swarms of a tiny insect, and something else that might be moths. The bug spray is doing the trick, but the realization comes to Adam that they left it back in the car, and what is on them will wash off when they swim. They'll be eaten alive afterwards. There is no breeze, and the night has suddenly gotten warm, maybe the warmest night they've had so far. He can feel sweat building between his body and the backpack, which he lifts away from his back to let the air in. Why's it so hot, Adam wonders aloud. It's the water, Teddy says, aiming the light. And Teddy is right: from the opaque, rainbow-slick surface, around little bits of swamp grass breaking through, wisps of steam are rising. We're getting close then, Adam whispers. He kneels on the rough boards and pushes two fingers into the dark water. It's not *that* warm, he says. It had better be better than this. Look at that, Teddy says, thrusting his beam of light at the surface. Adam looks, not asking what he is supposed to see. Teddy inhales a wordless *wow*, but Adam still can't see anything. He straightens and keeps walking, taking the lead despite having no light. Did you see it? asks Teddy, running after him, his boots too loud on the boards. What? whispers Adam. The fish, Teddy says, making no sense. No way did you see a fish, Adam says. There's fucking steam coming off the water. Fish couldn't live in that. He laughs, noticing the sudden cruelty in his voice. They'd get cooked, he adds more reasonably, putting a kind hand on Teddy's shoulder. Maybe they've evolved to handle it, says Teddy simply. Yeah, maybe, says Adam. Now he, too, has stopped being quiet. When he turns, he thinks he sees something glowing back at the trailhead. His neck tenses, and for a moment he is too frightened to say anything or even to nudge Teddy. It may have been the distant swing of headlights, something entering the trailhead carpark. More likely it was just a car passing along the highway. Whatever it was, it is no longer there. They keep walking, a little faster, not too fast. The boots they have been wearing for the last ten days get heavier, the promise of water whispering in Adam's ears. There's only one narrow boardwalk, nowhere to go but onwards or back toward the light, which may not even have been a light. He turns again and lets Teddy's footsteps go on without him. He stares back into the gloom, pulling each of the shoulder straps away from his body and scratching his chemical-coated skin. This may be what giving up feels like, trampling your own instincts, following a bad idea into a dead end, for no other reason than to please somebody else. But he agreed to it, so he might as well do it.

TEDDY IS THE one who initiates it, after struggling out of his greasy jeans. He wants this to feel mythical, pure, with no mediation between his body and the thick, dark water. Despite everything, he has not managed to destroy the childish belief that he can submerge himself and then come to the surface in some way changed. Water is always promising that. Of course he doesn't tell Adam what to do, but once he says Fuck this, I'm taking everything off, he has issued a challenge of sorts. Adam can follow along or not, but any objection to nakedness would only point the finger at himself. Ever since puberty, only very few boys would let themselves be seen before and after gym class, neither Teddy nor Adam among them. They wrapped towels around their bodies before dropping their boxers in the locker room, they jumped into the river in their underwear and afterwards stood on opposite sides of the truck while drying themselves. Teddy senses that they are beyond that now, having burst through whatever wall it was. He has seen Adam's junk once or twice, and their walks away from each other to piss have gotten shorter and shorter. In any case, it's pretty dark without the camera light, and they can only see the outlines of things, like the end of the boardwalk and a warning sign Teddy was careful not to read when he passed it with the light. It's more built up here than he imagined. Some institution has come along and prepared the place to receive visitors. There is even a small changing cabin, a place for the kind of privacy Teddy and Adam no longer need. He imagines being here in winter, being warm to the neck but with snow stinging his face, snowflakes dying as they reach the water. All of these contradictions, and no use for them. He piles his clothes beneath the sign, catching a final whiff of his boots. And it is mythical, it is pure. The moon has descended into the trees, but the water seems to shimmer with silver vapour. It is like an enchanted pool in a fairy tale, the kind you can never leave once you're in it because it slowly paralyzes you with pleasure. There is also a very faint smell of something sulphurous, which Teddy decides he enjoys. Fun and games, Adam says while flicking the water with his toes, and without looking Teddy knows his friend is naked too. Side by side, they work their way in slowly, as if it were cold water and needed getting used to. In fact, it is almost too hot on Teddy's thighs. Adam is scooping handfuls and splashing them into his armpits. Their chests and shoulders seem to glow before finally disappearing to the sound of emptying lungs. The two boys, or men, wade and then swim a little distance apart. Teddy rubs himself in the important places. The chaffed parts of him sting, but he doesn't care. Adam sighs with what sounds like delirious pleasure. About time, he says. So good, Teddy says, then puts his head under, his eyes squeezed shut. The water isn't so deep that he can't touch the pleasantly slimy bottom, which gets hotter when he digs his toes into it. He exhales enough to free his body of buoyancy, and for a few seconds just bobs there, submerged.

When Teddy finally surfaces, Adam is floating on his back with his arms stretched out, three points of dark hair making a sort of triangle, an arrow down. Welcome back, Theodore, he hears Adam say as he wipes the wet hair from his eyes. He has water streaming across his ears and only just catches the words. What did you say? asks Teddy. Adam says, I said welcome back. But did you call me Theodore? Yeah, Adam says, doubt in his voice now. Teddy propels himself backwards through the water and groans. You dumbass—my name isn't Theodore, Teddy says. What do you mean? says Adam. It's Edward, says Teddy. I mean, it isn't, I hate Edward, but that's what my parents called me. Teddy is short for Edward. Teddy can be Edward? asks Adam, confused. I thought it was like the American president. What the fuck, Teddy says lovingly. This whole time you didn't know my name. Adam splashes an arc of water with a skimming hand. There is a silence long enough to make Teddy worry he has hurt Adam's feelings, then Adam says, I was only called Adam because my dad was mad at my mom. That's what my grandma told me, anyway. My mom wanted to call me Peter, Adam says, and my dad didn't like it. He agreed to go along with it, but then I had some kind of heart thing when I was born, and they said there was a chance I'd die. And at the last minute my dad changed his mind and when he filled in whatever form you have to fill in he wrote *Adam*. He only told my mom about it after it was too late. Apparently for the first few months she still called me Peter, but he won in the end. Teddy is silent, listening, only his head breaking the surface of the water. Which one of them told you all that? he asks eventually. I told you, Adam says. My grandma. Who knows if it's true. She said my mom just gave up eventually. Peter, Teddy says, trying it out. Nope. Doesn't fit. But names are stupid anyway, Adam says. You get given them before anyone knows if they'll suit. I guess so, Teddy replies. He has never had cause to think that the person might fit around the name rather than the other way around. Grace is a pretty name, Adam says out of nowhere, in that tone he has that can make Teddy suddenly uneasy, unsure of what's coming next. Adam says, What's your mom's name again? Elizabeth, Teddy says. What's yours? But Adam has ducked below the water and when he surfaces he's several metres away, at the other end of the narrow pool. Anyway, fuck them, Adam says. Fuck them all. Time's up. It'll be light soon. And he is right about that, at least. Already Teddy can see the steam rising from the water in a way he couldn't when they arrived. Wait, he says. I want to wash my underwear. Okay, Adam says. Toss me mine too then. Gross, I'm not touching yours, Teddy says. But out of the water, with the air pleasant on his cooling skin, he knows he will. He will do whatever Adam asks. He feels drops running between his shoulders, a dull itch behind his knees and in the crooks of his arms and between his thighs, where sweat and dirt have gathered for so many days. He stands there for a few moments, watching the steam drifting from his arms. He should have brought some water. Adam has some in his bag, which is next to the rifle, which is wrapped in the silver tarp. Dawn is building beyond the trees, but here it is still safe. He hears Adam blowing his nose into his hand as he picks up both pairs of underwear and lobs them into the water. Adam has his back to Teddy, who can see the acne between his friend's shoulder blades. It looks painful, like it's bled recently. No wonder Adam is always contorting his arms to scratch back there. Some amount of Adam's blood will be in the water. Teddy doesn't yet know how it will happen, but he is suddenly certain that he does not want to leave this place, does not want to get back into the car. He looks along the boardwalk, as though he hopes someone will appear, a person he could side with, with whom he could agree that Adam is frightening and his body disgusting, a person who might reassure Teddy that anyone would have done what he did when faced with the same situation. But Teddy is alone, or thinks he is until he remembers the camera in the pocket of his pants.

HOW DO YOU know something behind you is watching? You just do. Your body tells you with a subtle tightening, neck and shoulders forcing a choice, to turn and look or go on as before, pretending you have not noticed. Nature gives everyone this extra sense but only activates it in exceptional situations. Maybe it has been decided that Adam should know about this. In the strengthening light he is sure, even without turning, that Teddy is filming him. So he does what anyone would do: he acts natural, pulls his stomach in, puts hands protectively on hips, and half turns so as to be captured in profile, staring into the trees. From the corner of his eye he at first only sees Teddy's arms, jutting like the handles on a trophy or an urn. With his elbows out like that, Teddy could almost be pissing. He is still shirtless, Adam senses, wearing his towel like a skirt, a slit running up past his knee. He is holding the camera at his pelvis and sucking Adam inside the aperture. As Adam tries to determine his next move, he feels the weight of being committed to a medium. This version of himself, here and now, is going to stand for the whole. What, after all, are they going to think when they watch this, after the fact? But Adam is too well trained to feel desolation, panic, or shame.

Something else rises in him, the only remaining winning move, the unbeatable one. They will say he was sick, a psycho. They will blame him for what has already happened and what is still coming. They will convince themselves not to worry, because this boy had pain in his heart, and had done for a long time. A broken boy cannot teach us anything about ourselves, they will think. So they will go defencelessly on until it is too late, and it is exactly this that makes Adam feel like dancing. Because what does he care? He has upheld his part of the bargain. He is glad, now, that he didn't bring the book with him; it doesn't belong here. He is beyond all that now, ready to make his own contribution. And his contribution is this: he raises one arm to the horizontal and begins an awkward shifting of weight between his legs, a march or a dance, as the water level moves up and down his hips, not quite revealing his pubic hair. He spins to face Teddy, or the camera, then yelps as he throws himself for the water to catch. Teddy is laughing now, but silently, not wanting to be present on the recording. The film will get shaky here, its unsteadiness the only trace of an accomplice, somebody behind the camera. Adam kicks to deeper water and watches light rising on the treetops. He dares himself to picture how it will end, who will go first and who will be trusted to remain there, alone. But he cannot see it yet. Give him an hour or two to work up to it. Let him submerge himself in the sticky mineral water, let him exhale and sink until his toes stir the silty bottom and nothing is urging him upwards again.

When he finally surfaces, Teddy is still filming, aiming at the sky and the looming sunrise. As Adam steps into shallower water,

Teddy trains the camera on him once more and says, What do you want to say? He is naked on camera now, but doesn't care. He pictures a pair of hands deftly dealing cards into two neat piles, and a woman's face made up of a hundred tiny lines. He rejoices in his audience of police, psychologists, parents, posters, everyone who would use him to feel safer in themselves. And determined to give them nothing, he turns to Teddy once more, mouthing a silent string of nonsense that will have them trying to read his lips, desperate for meaning.

DESPITE HIS MISFORTUNE, he is not an unhappy man. He moves from week to week, wearing into the ruts of his routine. He wakes up, urinates, eats breakfast, defecates, shaves, showers. He can work without forcing himself, and earns more than enough for someone with neither mortgage nor dependants. His work is performed in the part of his house he calls the office, which comprises a sunless room that the previous occupants, an elderly couple, used as their dining room, and an adjoining vestibule with its own door onto the driveway. I have the shortest commute in the country, he says. He enjoys saying. More than once he has joked to a client that he leaves his house each morning and enters his office from the outside. Of course he never actually does this, nor does anyone he tells believe it. It is a good joke; the image is effective without having to be true. He has his bad days, when a spiteful melancholy kindles in him, and with it the urge to seek out somebody who might witness his misfortune, perhaps feel the weight of it themselves, but for the most part he manages to keep the mechanism of his life well lubricated, so as to mesh without scraping. He exercises, eats pretty well, drinks pretty well. He eats blueberries with watery low-fat yogurt and a dark dash of syrup. He is scrupulous about his teeth.

In the summer months, he kayaks. His body is in good shape for fifty, never mind that nobody since Elizabeth has seen or touched it. He himself sees it and believes in the strength of which it still seems capable, its patient potential. He kayaks in neoprene shorts and a windbreaker over an old woollen sweater, his hat fastened with adjustable, elasticated cord. On windy mornings, the cord and its toggle dig into the soft place between his chin and throat. Sometimes he surprises himself by how far and how long he paddles, clear across the bay from the beach where he has parked, skirting the river mouth to the disused cannery. Waves clap at his little craft, water runs from the blades to chill his hands. Sometimes conditions are enough to fill him with adrenaline and doubt, and afterwards he stands on the beach hot with delayed fear, staring at what he has just done. He looks across the choppy waves to the distant cannery, which looms out of the forest and even from a distance seems ready to collapse at any moment. The sensation of solid ground after a long paddle sends pleasant electricity into his knees. He grunts as he lifts the kayak back onto his car's roof racks. He exhales as if to an audience. For a day or two afterwards, his muscles burn nicely.

He is one of those whom tragedy has touched indirectly. It is nothing to make a song and dance about, he tells himself, though he is willing to drop hints to anyone who asks. I used to be close with Edward Anscombe's family, he says. With the mother especially—Elizabeth. He adds this detail with what he believes is subtlety. It's been hell for her, he says. Changed their lives forever. And mine too, in a way. When he has said these things, he has taken a slight, sad pleasure in them. He is careful not to spell anything out, to leave plenty to the imagination. The people he tells must think: There's more to that than he's letting on. And they must think: But he seems happy enough, all things considered. Not unhappy, anyway. They may even recognize the quality of fortitude and add it to their impressions of him.

Once a week, a woman arrives. She parks her car behind his and cleans his house from top to bottom. She is a good worker, quiet and thorough. He is careful not to watch her work, though he is friendly when she arrives. He puts the agreed amount in one of the envelopes he uses for his work. The woman's husband is dead, though he cannot recall how he came to know this. At some point she begins bringing her daughter each week, who is five or six or seven and who sits quietly at his kitchen table while her mother works. He has no particular interest in children, despite how close he believes he came to being a stepfather. Why then does he try so hard to charm her? Mainly he wants reassurance that he does not frighten the girl, his cleaner's daughter. She does not seem to be frightened by him. She climbs onto his usual chair without saying a word, unpacking books and coloured pens from a backpack while her mother kneels on his linoleum floor to retrieve the cleaning supplies. Watching the girl one morning, he realizes with wonder that it makes no difference at all to her, that she could do her drawing at any table in the world, so long as her mother was nearby and she had her apple juice and her pink backpack full of treasures. She is not too shy to stare back at him, a cold and curious look, as though he were a specimen behind glass. Her hair is cut in a sloping fringe that is probably her mother's work; it is a little too high on her forehead, he thinks. He retreats into his office and stays there until he hears the woman's car start. Then he slowly reclaims his space, walking from room to room until he reaches the kitchen. The smells are chemical, sterile, reassuring. Later, flossing his teeth amid a scent of lemon bleach, he decides to buy the little girl a present. After all, he has plenty of money, more than he knows what to do with, certainly more than the girl's mother has.

The following evening, he finishes his work and drives half an hour to a toy store he knows is open late. He wanders aisles of packaging, passing endless pairs of oversized, unblinking eyes. He begins to feel overwhelmed. Worse, he can imagine somebody watching him, questioning his motives. Everything he inspects looks unforgivably cheap, and he does not know the girl's exact age, which suddenly seems like vital information. He tries to remember what he has seen emerging from the pink backpack. A horse, he recalls, its glossy mane and tail an unnatural colour, blue or green, designed to be petted and groomed. It is nearly closing time; the only attendant has abandoned her register and is neatening items in what must be the boys' section: make-believe weapons, industrial vehicles in miniature, a cabinet of menacing black drones. There are no other customers, and the bright, thin music is driving him crazy. He decides to cut his losses and chooses a plastic horse that looks similar to the one the girl already has. It was either that or walk out empty-handed, he thinks as he drives home, wondering what he has just done, and why. He stops at a gas station that is cheaper than the one nearer his house and fills up, after which he feels calmer.

The next week, the woman comes without her daughter. When he enquires, she tells him her mother usually looks after the girl, that her mother has been unwell but is now better, well enough to take care of her granddaughter again. As the woman begins to clean his house he wavers, unsure whether to give the gift, the plastic horse, to the mother or wait until he sees the daughter again. He is faced with the further problem that the woman may notice the toy in the course of her cleaning, and might find it odd if it is later presented to her as a gift. While the woman is busy in his kitchen, he goes into his office and closes the door. He takes the horse—which is more anthropomorphic than he noticed at first, with eyelashes and the hint of a smile around its muzzle—and tucks it in the back of his filing cabinet. He does not see the girl again, and when he asks after her he feels that the woman, his cleaner, is guarded or even suspicious. But perhaps he is just imagining this.

On the afternoon of his fiftieth birthday, he is wrangling the ironing board from the closet when he remembers a joke his mother once made, at his expense. Ron, she had said, in a voice hollowed out by radiation, if you don't settle down and have kids, there'll come a day when you regret it. Her face was set, her lipstick immaculate as it always is in his memory. Before he could answer her, her smile turned wicked and she added: But what's one day of regret, in a lifetime of bliss? The extra breath she needed after the word *regret* made her timing even better. He laughed, partly because it was funny and partly to drown out her own gasping laugh. He pours distilled water into the iron and remembers her hands advancing on his as the laughter died, the knots of bone inside the hands, her ring with the opaque, coral-coloured stone. A day you don't laugh's no good day, she said. She used to say. Another time that winter they were walking inchmeal through her garden when she called him over to show him something beneath the crabapple tree. She was pointing into the weeds beside the tree and saying, Ron, down there, do you see it? She had her voice back that day; it came and went, and each time it came he was fooled into thinking she was getting better. As he bent over to look, she stepped back and with surprising strength shook the branch above him. A ridge of half-melted snow fell across his head and inside his collar. He knows now, ironing a shirt on his fiftieth birthday, that this was kindness. She had wanted to hear him say the word *Mom* the way he had as a teenager. She had wanted him to be her child for a moment, instead of her caregiver.

The shirt is still warm when he puts it on. It seems not to want to touch more of him than it has to. Perhaps he is thinning. He would have preferred to walk along the foreshore with Elizabeth today, to order wine in a restaurant, to be smiled at, even laughed at, by her. He would have preferred to be someone who went without saying. He would have preferred to have sex. But circumstances being what they are, he is having drinks with his friend Freeman, at the regular place. He is lucky even to get this much: Freeman runs a bakery and probably woke up at two o'clock this morning but has agreed to nap after work and join him for the evening. Birthday privilege, Freeman called it on the phone, a teasing smile in his voice.

When they were foundering, Elizabeth pointed out that their relationship began not long after his mother died. He cannot now remember exactly where the comment came from, only that it was an accusation he resented. Okay, Sigmund, he either replied or wished he had, later, when he replayed the conversation in his mind. What made it inexcusable was that she must have seen it that way the whole time, must have thought of him as a drowning man reaching blindly for any offered hand. And yet she had gone along with it anyway. And what did that say, exactly, about her own motives? He assumed he would have a chance to ask her this, to take back some of what he had said, to repair things generally. Then the tragedy happened, and Elizabeth, as she had been, disappeared overnight. He was swept along by it just like everyone else who knew the family. He even spent some mute hours in Elizabeth's house, in the same room as her husband, grasping for the mislaid role of family friend. He told himself Elizabeth needed him, and he felt at least useful if not much more. What he was really doing was trying to assert his relevance, and after a few months she asked him to stop. She asked him kindly, almost romantically. She needed it for the sake of her family, needed it without wanting it, she told him, as if he were the one whose situation called for handling with gloves. So he gallantly returned to his solitude, and began hinting to anyone who would listen that Elizabeth had been on the point of upending her life for him, that if it had not been for the boy . . . He had never thought much about the word *stepfather* while there was a chance of his becoming one. He had no particular desire to do whatever it was they did. Grace and Teddy were nearly adults, after all, and there was no reason to assume anything particular would be expected of him. And so he remained safely hypothetical until it was too late, after which eagerness flooded into the space left behind. Her children had been part of why he loved her, part of what he loved about her. They would have come with the territory, and it was territory. It was land he had been promised, on which he was to have built his life. Once it was too late, *stepfather* arrived on his tongue with surprising ease. It was a failure of community and of family, he would say. He would almost enjoy saying. And I include myself in that. I know I could have done more. I could have been more. Edward Anscombe himself looms on the periphery of such conversations, free, like any ghost, to come and go. When he thinks of Teddy he cannot help seeing the ubiquitous photo, a profile picture enlarged to the brink of distortion and placed, alongside his friend's face, beneath every headline and on every news report. The eyes looking beyond the camera at something, or at nothing, elbows cocked and hands behind his neck, and that careless smile, the same as his mother's, as though all of time were his. He has tried, while staring at the photograph, to recognize something there, a man within the boy, but he cannot; or perhaps he turns away from it each time he is on the brink.

*

Because he was born in July, and because he lives on the town's eastern margin, driving to the bar means looking into the liquid evening sun. Even with the visor down there are times when he cannot quite see the oncoming traffic and trusts his memory to keep him on the right side of the line. Inside, he sits at the bar to wait for Freeman, who is forgivably late. Andrea is working tonight. She is his favourite; her father used to be one of his clients. She is twenty-three or twenty-four or twenty-five, and wears her jeans rolled to reveal what he can only describe as statement socks. Nice socks, he says each time he sees her. And she thanks him with the same patient laugh, their little routine. Today's have pineapples. When she reaches across the bar to take his credit card, he notices for the first time a straight line tattooed up the soft inside of her arm. It must be new, he thinks, though he decides not to ask. She might ask him if he likes it, and he does not. She opens his first bottle with a cool snap, and he watches her slide the flat steel opener as far as it will go into her back pocket. As she turns to face him his eyes shift quickly to the television. She gives him his beer then retreats to where she left her phone, out of range of casual conversation.

There is rugby on the television, at least he is pretty sure that's what it is. A badge in the corner of the screen says it's the World Cup. It's being beamed in from some distant, sunny time-zone where large men glisten and collide. There is a black team and a white team. Some of the players are wearing tape around their heads, as though an injury has been treated hastily. The sound is off, but he can feel their grunts as they hurl themselves at one another. Every so often the referee seems to give somebody a talking to, and they stand patiently with hands on hips, waiting for permission to go on. He sips his beer and watches one of the white men cradling the ball in the front of his shirt. Without knowing anything about the sport, he can tell something is about to happen. The rest of them line up in formation as the man with the ball steps off the field and holds it above his head, mutely shouting in close-up. The others plant their feet and look hungry. When the man with the ball finally lobs it, two of the biggest white players surround a teammate, grabbing him by the thighs and hoisting him skywards. The teammate reaches an implausible height, and with outstretched hands catches the ball at the immaculate peak of its arc, clutching it to his chest before landing flawlessly. Seeing this, he cannot help glancing around the bar, to check if anyone else is watching. Andrea is looking at her phone; a couple of tradesmen types are laughing loudly at something one of them has just said. He feels the simultaneous pleasure and grief of having witnessed something remarkable with nobody to remark to. But when he looks back at the television, it has come to nothing: both teams are simply grappling on the grass again, as though the miracle of the flying man never happened.

Old man, Freeman almost shouts, landing a slap on one of his shoulder blades. Stand up while I embrace you. Freeman is in jeans and a T-shirt; he has greying hair past the ears and is tall enough that his paunch looks odd on him, a blip between legs and chest. It is a recent thing, and his wardrobe has not yet caught up. They hug. He almost thanks Freeman for coming, but stops himself. Did you nap? he asks instead. Freeman shakes his head and says, No time. I had another meeting with the wedding-cake woman—we're going to be partners. Freeman, that's great, he replies. Sounds like we ought to celebrate.

They switch to a booth, and he listens to Freeman's plans for empire, seemingly cribbed from the wedding cake designer's sales pitch. Nobody throws more cash around than the bride and groom's parents, Freeman says. It's like they think you're the one who decides how the marriage will work out. And this woman's sister is a photographer, so between us we'll have the whole racket stitched up. He is happy to see Freeman so energetically optimistic. It is a positive development. When it is his turn to speak, he says, So you're saying marriage might be the secret to your success after all? Freeman laughs, spreads his hands wide on the tabletop, shakes his head. They can joke about this now. He has watched his friend's life fall apart, and watched him rebuild it. He was once friends with both of them, Freeman and his ex-wife. For a while it was a typical friendship between a couple and a single person, both sides taking comfort in the knowledge that they were not missing out on much. In hindsight he was always slightly uncomfortable around Renée, who talked as if something distasteful was forever going unmentioned and she was disappointed in him for not just coming out and saying it, whatever it was. By the end, it was staring him in the face. He could not say for certain that Freeman had been violent with Renée, but he had gone out of his way to preserve his ignorance. He had once stood beside his friends' smoking barbecue with a lukewarm can in his hand, waiting for the two of them to come back from inside the house. Renée had gone to change the baby, and Freeman had followed her. He could hear chairs shifting, voices that rose before going silent for seconds at a time. He could not make out the words, but something, a palm or fist, was beating out the rhythm of a point being made. He wanted to get into his car and drive away, not to embarrass them by witnessing, but his keys and things were where he had left them on the kitchen table. Another part of him knew his friend might need to be stopped from doing something he would regret. He stood uselessly there and raked coals, swallowed the starchy dregs of his beer, and waited until the sounds solidified and he was afraid for the baby, who did not even seem to be crying, or else her cries were being swamped. When he finally reached the kitchen, he caught them in a dance. One of Renée's wrists was wrapped in Freeman's fist, her body had unfurled as though she had been spun on the dancefloor. He said something anemic like Play nice, you two, something otherwise said to children. Freeman let go of her, throwing up his hands and walking past him out the door, leaving him with Renée's shuddering back and the mass of black curls that obscured her face. He was afraid that if she turned toward him, he would see something that required action. Then he heard a car start and was thankful for the simpler task of preventing Freeman from driving drunk. He left Renée facing the wall, and by the time he returned, having failed to stop Freeman driving away, she was dry-eyed and busy, with Merilee on her shoulder. She asked him, he remembers, if he wanted to take some food home. He never questioned that she would wipe herself clean like that, and spare him having to ask her something he didn't want answered. It was just one of those miracles that seem to happen to a man now and then. But he can still ask himself why he never said anything about it to Freeman, after that or any other occasion. The closest he came was a few days later, in the bar they are both sitting in now. He said, I guess you don't want to talk about it. All Freeman had to do was agree.

Another miracle happened when he found out about Freeman's custody hearing. He was certain he would have to tell a judge what he had seen. Renée could have demanded it, but didn't. By that stage he no longer spoke to her, so could not ask her why even if he had wanted to. The hearing was at the family court, a two-hour drive away. Expecting the worst, he told Freeman to meet him at the bar afterwards. But he could tell as soon as his friend walked in that things had gone well. Freeman ordered an uncharacteristic Sprite and told him that the judge, a woman, had torn both him and Renée apart. Excoriated us, Freeman said, as though he had picked the word up at the hearing. The judge had said they should both be ashamed of themselves for putting their anger ahead of their daughter's well-being. She ordered them to do better, to try harder. The judge, apparently, had used their daughter's name over and over, sometimes twice in a single sentence. What kind of childhood are you giving Merilee? How will Merilee look back on this when Merilee is an adult with her own life and issues of her own? What would Merilee say if I asked her what her parents are like? I am not the judge you need to worry about, the judge had said. And now Freeman has joint custody, and wedding cakes, and his beer belly, and afternoon naps. He seems to enjoy fatherhood more now that his daughter is old enough to talk, old enough to worship him.

The men look at their hands while they talk, at the horizontal liquid in their bottles. Or they look past each other, weighing the value of what the other cannot see. After letting Freeman tease him about being middle-aged, he says, I haven't heard you complain about your back in a while. They've got me on oxycodone, Freeman says proudly. Jesus, he can't help saying, isn't that a bit full-on—and addictive? The pain is pretty full-on too, Freeman says, straightening himself as though remembering a doctor's order. You should come kayaking, he replies. The stronger your core is, the less strain on your back. Freeman grins and says, Or I could take the magic pill and stay lazy. They are expert skirters of an issue; soon they have moved on to the problems they read about and have opinions on, matters in which they are powerless and therefore blameless. But aren't we problem-solvers by nature, Freeman asks. Otherwise what is it we do all day? We create more than we solve, he replies. Exactly, Freeman says, spreading his arms like a point should be awarded. This is what I'm saying: we're *creative*.

One drink later he leaves Freeman at the table and goes outside to return a call from his brother. His nephew appears on the screen in pajamas, dancing to his own breathy performance of Happy Birthday. We won't keep you, his brother tells him. This one just wanted to say happy birthday before bed. Sleep tight, buddy, he tells the screen, I'll come visit you soon. Have a good night, his younger brother says. Have a crazy one for me. After he hangs up he stares at the phone screen for a few seconds, at its ordered grid of icons, then he finds Elizabeth's number and dials it. The saw-tooth ringtone runs three times against his ear before he hangs up. He kicks a pebble through the parking lot and is pleased to hear it click on a stranger's car. For a moment he feels capable of pure, thoughtless malice, the way a child is. He is angry at Teddy, and at Elizabeth for believing in her son's victimhood despite all the evidence. He is angry at himself for not taking what he wanted while it was on offer. Then like an antidote comes the reminder that he is no longer attached to that damaged family, that responsibility was never his to take, that he—in Freeman's terrible but unintentional phrasing—had dodged a bullet. Two women have gotten out of their hatchback and are taking the long way around the parking lot to avoid him. It's too cold to stand there any longer. His jacket is inside and his shirt is too loose; the night is getting underneath it. He waits long enough that the two women will not think he is following them, then goes back inside. Freeman is waiting with two glasses of whiskey, doubles. Teri has joined Andrea behind the bar and is smiling over at them, at him. Happy birthday, her smile says. Sorry, Freeman, he says, putting his phone face-down between them. Freeman drums the table and says, Hey, birthday privilege. Who were you on the phone to? My nephew, he says. Well, no driving from here on out, Freeman says. You can stay at my place, okay? Sounds like what I deserve, he replies, as they bring their glasses together a little too forcefully.

The bar has changed since they arrived. It's finally dark outside, and the cheerful neons above the counter shine brighter. There's a constant jostle of laughter, glass, and colliding pool balls. Andrea has turned the music up, forcing those around tables to lean closer. In the other room, where the pool table is, younger voices compete for air time, race each other to punchlines. The rugby has finished; now the screen shows a woman's lips moving above the caption POSTSEASON HOPES FADE. Freeman, he asks, how long have you been awake? Freeman grins, squinting at his watch.

He spots Grace just as he puts his weight against the heavy men's room door. He hasn't seen her for two years, but it is unmistakably her. She is at the centre of the loud group in the back room by the pool table. He doesn't know how she could have come in without him noticing, or without her spotting him. All through his time at the urinal her face is frozen in the glimpse he got, surrounded at a table, head down, not talking but clearly being talked to, talked about. She was smiling like somebody determined to enjoy herself, which makes him pity her. His clumsy mind tries to game it out: she was accepted to a college on the other side of the country. He wouldn't have sent her away from her family after what had happened, but it was none of his business by that stage. Who knows, maybe she wanted to go. Maybe having to come back is harder. It must be summer break, he thinks while he waits for the last drops to straggle out of him. I should say hello, he thinks. I should ask how she is, how Elizabeth is. She must not have noticed me when she came in. As he thinks these things he tips gently forward on his toes, until he feels a mild stretch in his calves and his forehead is resting on the cold bathroom tiles. He sees his nephew dancing for his brother's phone camera, showing off for his uncle and trying to push back bedtime. How desperate kids are to stay awake. He imagines Teddy charging through the trees, his bloodless fingers gripping, of all the implausible things, a weapon. He remembers the infamous interview with Adam Velum's father, who, he is pretty sure, is the same man who sold him his kayak. How the father had predicted what would happen. I know my son, the man had said into the camera, tears in his eyes though not actually crying. And I don't think he's coming back. How lonely they all were. Teddy without a friend left in the world. He sees him running through summer undergrowth, along that last stretch of hillside to the place where they found his body, nearly a kilometre from the other one. He had put a thousand metres between himself and his friend, and then stopped. Nobody knew why, or what to do about it.

On his way back to his table, he stares openly at Grace. She is talking now, though still looking down at her own patch of table, as her friends' heads bow in a ring around her. Another young woman has put a hand at the centre of her back, though she does not look distressed. She looks like somebody who is being congratulated for something but does not believe she deserves the attention. He stares as though willing her to notice him, wanting her eyes to flick upwards and bloom with recognition. But when Grace does look up from the tabletop, she does not see him, or perhaps chooses not to. Whatever she is in the middle of saying runs on without pause. Her hair is shorter, tucked behind an ear. She looks more like Elizabeth than she did two years ago, and seeing her older echoes dully with a knowledge that Elizabeth herself is older now, just as he is older. Then he is pulled into

Freeman's orbit. Freeman has not ordered more drinks as he hoped he would, but is tenting his fingers and staring with heavy eyes. Maybe we should head out, Freeman says, before he has even sat back down. That's Grace, he replies, as breezily as he can manage. She must be back from college. She's been through a lot, Freeman says. We all have, he replies, and when Freeman makes a face he quickly adds: Not like that, obviously. He has overplayed his hand and is shamefully aware of it. Come on, Freeman tries again. I'd better just go say hi, he replies, make sure she's doing okay. Better not, Freeman says. She's been away at university, he says, as though this is some sort of counterargument. We never had the chance to talk properly when it all happened. She looks happy, Ron, Freeman says. Let her be with her friends. He tries to scoff at this, but it comes out wonky. He would have driven her places, he thinks, given her advice, lent her money he knew he'd never see again. He could have proved his mother wrong and had a family after all. You don't understand, he says, she's practically my stepdaughter. Freeman leans across the table and puts a hand on his wrist. No she isn't, Ron. A moment goes by before Freeman releases him and says, How about this? How about we get a shot before we go? One for the road.

He is sober enough to enjoy fingering his keys on the walk back to Freeman's house: the flat dimpled blade of the car key, the lighter, jagged one that fits his front door, the plastic fob that opens his garage. These are things he knows. When they pass his car in the lot, he lightly touches a roof rack. I'll go kayaking tomorrow, he says. Do my penance for tonight. Freeman says, You're a better man than I am, I'm going to sleep until Monday. He replies: You can use my old kayak if you want to come with me, work on that belly of yours. Freeman cups his bump and says, I work plenty hard on this belly. How do you think I got it so nice? It is a comfortable routine; they are each doing an impression of the man they hope they are. There are no streetlights on Freeman's street, and they walk the final fifty metres in darkness. As he waits for Freeman to open the front door, he holds his elbows in his palms and presses his thighs together. Come on, he says, laughing, I've got to piss. In the hallway he lists slightly, not quite a stumble, a misjudgment of his position in space. Standing and urinating, he again pictures Grace encircled by friends. Thank god for Freeman, he thinks. He would only have embarrassed himself. The call to Elizabeth he pushes, for the moment, from his mind.

When he gets back from the bathroom, he sinks into a faded beige couch. You can have Merilee's bed, Freeman calls from elsewhere in the house. Her comforter's tiny, but I have blankets somewhere. He nods to these words but does not reply. When Freeman's distant voice offers him a glass of water, he calls back, How about a drink? The carpet is worn through in places; the couch has a map-like stain over one cushion, juice maybe, a child's mistake. The television, too, is at odds with its cabinet; it faces the front door rather than the couch. He is irritated by these things, and by the fact that he is not in his own home. Freeman is now saying something about his daughter's schoolteacher being attractive as hell and how all she wants to do is play games on his phone. Merilee this must be, not the teacher. Freeman has booked her into swimming lessons, but she needs coaxing, she is afraid of the water. He grunts to show he is listening, leaning forward to carefully unlace one shoe. They are his good shoes, the ones he wears when he meets with a client, the ones he would wear if he were to go on a date. He thinks of Merilee Freeman in goggles, circumspect in the lukewarm shallows of a kids' pool. He thinks of the bridge between this town and Elizabeth's, the one the kids all jump from, and how his heart lurches when he drives past and sees them. He gives up on his shoes and tilts his head back until he is looking through the window upside down. He once saw Teddy on that bridge. Maybe the other kid was there too, apparently they went everywhere together that final summer. Elizabeth said she didn't know what Teddy saw in him. But you don't choose your friends, not really. They knock against you in the current and snare, and you either shake free or you don't. When he saw that the boy perched in the steel truss that afternoon was Teddy, it was fate. He had been with Elizabeth all morning, and now here was her son in need of a friendly word of advice, equal parts encouragement and caution. Or was it he himself who needed that? Here was the person who could restore his faith in what he and Elizabeth were doing, who could show him the future. He took his foot from the gas and pressed the button for the passenger window. He hoped whatever he was about to say would sound different coming from a non-parent. They could talk the way friends did, because that is what he wanted them to be. Teddy turned to stare at the now stationary car, standing perilously on the railing in what looked like his underwear. He remembers thinking that Teddy was a handsome kid, and Grace was certainly a pretty girl, and knowing this made Elizabeth even more beautiful to him. These children were part of why he loved her, he told himself. He turned the radio down and leaned across the passenger seat. What's up, he said to Teddy, who for a moment looked suspicious and said nothing. Remember me? Sure, Teddy said eventually. Hey. Because Teddy was standing on the railing, he had to duck slightly and tilt his head to see the boy's face. He felt suddenly foolish, unwelcome. The boy was looking down at him. There was the sound of another voice, somebody shouting up from the river. Now that he had Teddy's attention, he wasn't sure what to say. Anybody ever tell you how dangerous that is? he finally managed. Teddy laughed, or scoffed, a short sharp breath with voice in it, and said: We do it all the time. And from there it seemed the only way out of the situation was confederacy, so he said, Well, I won't tell your mother. He might have said *parents* rather than *mother*, but he didn't. He wanted Teddy to know who he was. The voice from below called out again, and Teddy turned to look over the edge. Be careful, Teddy, he said finally, and Teddy gave him an impatient wave without turning around. That was it. He drove off so he wouldn't have to watch the kid jump.

So you'd want me in their lives, he had said to her, either that or some other day. He wanted to understand what she planned to make of him, who he was supposed to be. They'd be in *my* life, she replied, suddenly frustrated, so they'd be in yours. It's not like you'd have a choice. I mean, is that okay? Of course, he said, worrying that it sounded hollow, not meaning it to sound hollow, but he was helpless. She had put him in a corner somehow. After a pause he didn't know how to fill, he added: Maybe we'll have one of our own. She laughed grimly and said, I hope you're joking, Ron. I'm joking, he said. Of course I am.

The sky through Freeman's window is empty except for a single slender tree, which inches back and forth with nauseating rhythm, upside down of course, because of how he is sitting. He closes his eyes to rid himself of the motion, and when he opens them again Freeman is kneeling at his feet. There is a sound he recognizes as the slipping of a shoelace. Freeman's hair is more obviously thinning from this angle, he notices. He feels a welcome palm on his Achilles, a brief pressure on the ridge of his foot, and then the shoe is gone, dolloping away beneath the coffee table. He laughs, or thinks he does, but Freeman is not smiling as he moves to the other shoe; his lips are plump with concentration, his hands working the way they probably work bread. Why is your TV like that, Freeman? he asks, mainly to prove he is awake. Freeman, still kneeling, looks briefly into his eyes. Like what? Facing out the door, he says. Oh, Freeman says, getting to his feet with a grunt of discomfort. Merilee can't stand the couch. I think her mom told her something about bed bugs and now she's terrified of it. She wants me to get a new one, but I figure I'll wait until she's past the age where she spills shit everywhere. So I give her a cushion and she sits on the floor. But maybe now with this wedding cake money coming in, I should just buy something. He looks up at Freeman, who is suddenly towering over him, and does not quite comprehend what has happened to his shoes, or what relevance the story of the cushion has. His socks are damp and tight on his shins. He doesn't want another drink anymore, that ship has sailed. He receives his blanket and follows Freeman into Merilee's room. A small coterie of animals eye the two men from the bed until Freeman sweeps them up in his arms. Sitting heavily down on the child's bed, he begins peeling off his socks. Freeman gives him a mock salute and says, Help yourself to anything tomorrow. And try not to wake me up? The toilet's loud, so maybe don't flush unless you have to?

Merilee's bed is plenty big enough for him; Freeman has obviously purchased it with the future in mind, for the teenager she will be in a few years' time. It will never end, he thinks. To make matters worse, he can smell her, a light smell that is probably mostly fabric softener. He listens to the toilet flushing, the hissing cistern, and a door clicking into its latch, and he is wide awake in the darkness.

In the pre-dawn, he wakes up freezing. The blanket has retreated somewhere, and the first thing he locates is the little girl's comforter, which leaves him exposed from the knees down. It is not yet light, but the window has a cautious glow to it. It is either tragic or blindingly funny to wake up in this bedroom aged fifty. Never you mind it, his mother used to say when as a child he scraped or bumped himself. What she really meant was grin and bear it. Deal with it. One of his hands has been crushed by his own skull; he tries to make a fist, groaning to either coax or mock the delinquent fingers. For a few minutes he tries to fool himself back to sleep by deflating his lungs in slow, smooth motions. He uses the trick often, but this morning it fails him. So he fishes the blanket from the floor and sits with it around his shoulders, his stomach snug against his bladder. The animals Freeman moved from the bed are now dead, just objects heaped on a little commode. She must be forever greeting and farewelling toys as she switches houses, he thinks. High on the opposite wall is a large green-glowing fairy he barely noticed last night, fading now as it nears the end of its shift. From its wand sprout dots, or stars. Below are some vacant rectangles of art, stuck above the plump plastic table. It is still too dark for him to make out what they are pictures of. He sits with his hands in his lap, needing to urinate, wanting water, waiting to understand what he is doing there, awake and uncomfortable. There is something depressing about the room, he realizes: it is half-hearted, too spare, a part-time bedroom. And worse, he can smell himself in it now, his sweat, feet, and farts polluting the clean child smell.

As the light sharpens, he becomes aware of the first cautious birds, and the pictures Merilee has drawn come into focus. He wonders whether she will have depicted her mother here in her father's house, or whether instinct has already taught her that everything is to be segregated, that she must learn to be two different people. There in the uppermost picture is what must surely be Freeman, a tall dash beside a smaller figure; and yes, there is the evident paunch, a crude bubble halfway down the stick figure. He smiles to himself, almost laughs. For a moment, he feels envy. How did that man, he wonders, get a second chance as good as this?

He leaves the toilet unflushed, which he finds distasteful, but Freeman will probably sleep for hours yet. He cannot remember where the light switch is in Freeman's kitchen, nor where glasses and mugs are kept. His first guesses reveal only teetering stacks of baking equipment, a set of scales with the needle showing the weight of what rests on top. He doesn't want to bring anything crashing down, so he settles for a small pot with a thick cylindrical handle, something for warming milk or melting butter. The kitchen window looks toward the river, and beyond that, just out of sight, the bay. He fills his pot and drinks, leaning over the stainless-steel sink as he tries to distinguish objects in Freeman's yard. Fog has risen from the water and is waiting for the sun to burn it away. The birds are getting louder. He raps four fingertips softly against the rim of Freeman's sink. The sound is gentle and barely metallic, its rhythm regular. To a child it is the make-believe sound of a horse, carrying its rider at a gallop. To an adult it signifies impatience. He creeps back to the little girl's bedroom, putting her bed to rights. Then to the couch, where he left his shoes. Where Freeman removed them, he recalls, though surely that moment of intimacy couldn't really have happened. He rebuttons his shirt and in two minutes he is passing sleeping cars and quiet houses. By the time he reaches the bar, the sun has cleared the rooftops and he feels faint warmth on his bare head. The bar is dark and silent. His is the only car still sitting shamefully in the lot. To reach it, he has to step over the memory of dialing Elizabeth's number. This was not the first time he has tried to contact her, despite his promise. At times she has let him unburden himself before gently ending the call. At times she has been angry. Lately, it is her voicemail on which he imposes. At least he did not leave a message. Perhaps that is progress. Perhaps every man turns boy on his birthday, amid the indulgence and attention. Birthday privilege. But when is it not a man's birthday?

He parks in the usual spot, and for a minute or more stands looking across the calm water. He is the only person in the scene, as far as he can tell: to be an early riser is to own the world. Even the dog-walkers are still in bed. There is hardly a breeze; the air is cold, but he knows he will be warm, too warm, once his body starts working. He walks to the edge of a dune and stains the sand with his urine, then unstraps the kayak. As he is lifting it down, he sees he has made a mistake. He has left the passenger door open, making it awkward to get the boat's nose clear of the car. He adjusts his grip, grunting as he forces it upwards over the door, and in doing so loses control of the stern. The fibreglass meets the ground with what may be a crack, hard enough to jar his hands. He swears, almost dropping it altogether. If he has broken it, he will go home unsatisfied. He will have to find a professional to fix it. His routine will be disrupted. Once it is laid out on the beach, he kneels at the stern and presses the way a doctor might, feeling for swelling or fractures. He shakes his head at his stupidity and his luck. Just to be sure, he drags the boat into the freezing water and pushes it below the surface. He silently counts to ten, after which his feet are numb and he is reassured. There is a faint streak of moisture, which may be condensation for all he knows, nothing to worry about.

The water is smooth, clear down to the pebbles with a hint of pink sky in it. As he sets off he watches two heavy birds, geese he thinks, flying low across the bay toward a common goal, perhaps home. His unwashed armpits itch, his stomach muscles tighten. After a few minutes the water has grown opaque and he is approaching the river mouth, from where the roof of Freeman's house is just visible. He tells himself it would be wise to stick closer to shore in case he has damaged the kayak after all. But he needs more than that this morning; he needs something that will feel like a payment in full. He reaches behind him to run a hand up the slimy bottom, still finding no more than a trace of water. Then he continues across the bay toward the far, uninhabited shore. Each stroke is progress; he is ridding himself of something unpleasant, expelling it through his lungs and pores. Somebody or something has given him the right to be his own judge, to determine his sentence, and this is what he has come up with. He pushes himself, working harder now than before, tearing at his deltoids and triceps, enjoying the urgency of breath. Aware of the slight bias in him, he works harder on the left side, keeping his course as true as possible. Sweat collects on his temples and forehead. The long ruin of the cannery inches up from the horizon. When he has done all he can do he rests, spinning a half circle to admire his strength and his solitude. His wake is a glassy wedge that dissipates within seconds, after which he is simply adrift on the swell, listening to the sound of his blood. Not far away is a flock of floating seabirds, a dozen or so pristine creatures with pied markings, heads folded neatly into their bodies. He looks first to the ruin, then again at the birds. He is glad to be ignored by them. It is the same thing as acceptance.

ACKNOWLEDGEMENTS

This book was written in public libraries in New York, Berlin, London, and Sydney; I'm grateful for these vital institutions and grateful to those who support them. Thanks to Jill Crawford, Rob Madole, Habib William Kherbek, Emily Waddell, Daisy Sainsbury, Elvia Wilk, Yan Ge, Gabriel Flynn, Lauren Oyler, Alexander Wells, Blake Thompson, Saskia Vogel, Martin Shaw, Chris Wellbelove, and everyone at The Novel Prize. Thomas Karshan's thinking and teaching on "play" will continue to be influential. Toby Litt's writing confirmed my suspicion that the Norman Mailer quote was apocryphal (so much the better). I'm extremely thankful to Dan Wells and Vanessa Stauffer at Biblioasis, Brigid Mullane at Ultimo Press, Will Rees at Peninsula Press, and Philip Gwyn Jones at Greyhound Literary. Thanks most of all to the wonderful Madeleine Watts.

Much of what I explore here began its slow formation many years ago during conversations with my friend Hugh Macready. This book is dedicated to his memory.

VIJAY KHURANA is a writer and translator from German. His work has appeared in *NOON*, the *Guardian*, the *Erotic Review*, and the *White Review Writing in Translation Anthology*, among others. He is currently completing a PhD in Creative and Critical Writing at Queen Mary, University of London. *The Passenger Seat*, his first novel, was shortlisted for the 2022 Novel Prize and selected as a Spring 2025 Indies Introduce pick by the American Booksellers' Association. He lives between Berlin and London.